WHEN EVERYONE
LOVED THE GAME

Published in the United States by
Beckham Publications Group, Inc.
P.O. Box 4066, Silver Spring, MD 20914

ISBN: 978-0-9816505-3-1

WHEN EVERYONE LOVED THE GAME

*A simple story, about a
complicated game in a simpler time*

Jim Shawn

THE Beckham
PUBLICATIONS GROUP, INC.
SILVER SPRING

To the thousands of Little League baseball players, um-pires, coaches and parents of players who are keeping alive the love of the game of baseball; and For Lacy, Devin and Brenda.

Chapter 1

"BALL FOUR!" THE UMPIRE, FATS Fitzsimmons, shouted.

There might have been a twinge of compassion in Fats' call. It was as if the home plate umpire was prepared to give the pitcher, Henry "Fast Ball" Harvey, the benefit of the doubt had the ball been close to the plate at all. Fats had been calling strikes in the major leagues for 27 years, even longer than Fast Ball's 23 years of throwing them. But this ball four was so far above the head of the third batter in the bottom of the second inning that there was no close call to make.

The leadoff batter for the Cardinals' half of the second inning was their shortstop, Rifle Dickinson, who had doubled to power alley in left and advanced to third on Lace Blackwell's infield single to the second base side. The walk of the third batter of the inning, Hank Pauling, had loaded the bases. Fast Ball already had given up three runs and five hits in the bottom of the first inning. A line drive double play had kept it from being worse. The start of the bottom of the second inning was not going much better.

Fast Ball turned his back on the plate, walked off the pitcher's mound toward second base, and reached down for the resin bag. Perspiration dropped off his left eyebrow as he sneaked a peek toward his visiting team dugout while bending over for the bag.

Russ Freeman, the manager for the Chicago Cubs, had his left foot on the top step of the visitors' dugout.

Fast Ball did not want to come out of the game, but he knew that he should. The Cubs could not afford to get much farther behind and have any hope of a comeback. It was too big a game to delay a pitching change. The only thing standing in the way of bringing in Lefty Owens, the Cubs' long reliever, was the friendship between Russ and Fast Ball.

Russ and Fast Ball had played minor-league ball together in Double-A for 1 year in the Cubs organization before they were called up to the major-league team. Russ had been a power-hitting first baseman, and Fast Ball was a hard-throwing right-handed pitcher. They were both 18 years old when they were drafted by the Cubs out of different high schools separated by 450 miles and three state boundaries. Russ was from Alabama. Fast Ball was from Texas.

Russ might have been as good a first baseman and home run hitter as Fast Ball had been a pitcher over the last 23 years, but a severe knee injury caused by a spring training collision at home plate just before his fifth season in the big leagues put an end to any hope Russ had of breaking the major-league record for most home runs by a first baseman.

To stay in baseball after his injury, Russ first tried to play winter ball in Mexico. After just two months in the Mexican League, he started coaching when he realized he couldn't push off his back leg hard enough to accelerate through the pitch to generate enough weight transfer to power the ball over the right field fence. Warning track power was not good enough to play first base for a major-league team, even the Cubs who had never won their division in the franchise's history.

Even though he could no longer play for the Chicago Cubs after his injury, Russ discovered that he loved to coach. Last year, the Cubs' front office fired their manager during the All-Star break and gave him his first chance as a major-league manager. He was a popular choice with the fans, with the media, and with the players.

The Cubs' players, an assortment of aging veterans and enthusiastic youngsters, played .500 ball during Russ's tenure as manager the prior year, and the promise of the current season had been enough for Fast Ball to want to come back one more time in hopes of winning ten or twelve games while providing a role model for the younger players, in particular, the young pitching staff.

Fast Ball had done substantially better than winning ten or twelve games. By the All-Star break this year, he was 14–6. After the All-Star break, however, Fast Ball's trademark pitch dropped in velocity from the mid-90s to the high-80s, and his reliable curve was fooling no one. He had won only two games since the break, and he had lost eight. His record stood at a still respectable 16–14 when he had taken the mound earlier in the day. If the Cubs could win today, they would be the National League East Division champions for the first time in the history of the world. But if they lost today, they would have to return home for a winner-take-all makeup game with the Cincinnati Reds, their longtime nemesis.

That was the situation as Russ stood with both feet on the top of the visitors' dugout. Two weeks earlier, he privately had considered releasing Fast Ball and calling up Fred Farley from the club's Triple-A team in Daytona. Fred was billed as the "Future Fast Ball" and had been pitching well of late after a slow start due primarily to a contract negotiation dispute. After rejoining the Triple-A club two months ago, Fred had won his last ten starts after losing his first two.

Turk McGhee, the Triple-A manager, had told Russ that Fred was ready, but Russ was concerned about bringing Fred up in such a pressure situation. Plus, he was hoping his longtime friend could win one more game to finish his career as a division champion to compensate for years of personal greatness spent on a mediocre team. But Fast Ball was not going to win this game. Russ had to take him out. Russ took his first, and hardest, step out of the top of the dugout and walked toward the mound.

Fast Ball had slowed down his preparation for the next batter to give Russ time to wade through his options and make the right choice. Fast Ball was through for the day, maybe for the year, and perhaps, for his career. He didn't like it any, but he knew his team's only chance to win the division today was to get him out of the game and bring in Lefty Daniels. Lefty had been warming up in the bullpen since the double by Rifle Dickinson. Lefty also had thrown a few pitches during the three-run first inning, so he was ready. Lefty had stopped throwing when Russ started walking toward the mound, and he waited to see what decision Russ would make.

"Henry," said Russ when he and the catcher, Legs Cooper, arrived at the pitching rubber (Russ had always called Fast Ball by his given name, not his nickname). "I've got to take you out."

"I know," said Fast Ball. "It's the right thing."

Fast Ball handed the ball to Russ, then looked his friend in the eyes with an expression of both appreciation and disappointment. After that, he pulled his cap way down low over his eyes and walked off the field. He wondered if it would be for the last time.

Lefty came in, and after a sacrifice fly to right field, he was able to get the next batter to ground into a double play, third to second to first, and the side was retired. Lefty had done his job, and the Cubs were still in the game, behind 4 to 0 after two full innings.

But the Cubs were unable to get anything going against the Cards' ace pitcher and lost the road game before a full house. You could almost hear a collective sigh of concern from every Cub fan in Chicago as the last out in the visitors' half of the ninth inning was made. The Cubs had lost; Fast Ball Harvey had failed. They were returning home for a one-game playoff against the dreaded Cincinnati Reds.

The Cubs' fans were loyal, and they supported their team with every ounce of enthusiasm they had. They were grateful to have a major-league team in their city.

Their stadium was called Wrigley Field in honor of the team's original owner. It was located in a business and neighborhood district easily accessible by public transportation to downtown Chicago. The Cubs' longsuffering fans cherished the stadium's odd angles and irregular distances from home plate to the outfield fences. Every local fan knew by heart the story of how Russ Freeman had hit the first pitch he ever saw as a major leaguer in a regular season game over the right field stands and into the picture window of a house across the street from the right field bleachers.

The Cub fans wanted to establish a winning tradition to go with their love of the game in Chicago. But it was hard to establish a winning tradition while finishing in the second division of the league as the Cubs had done 33 times. The Cubs had never finished first; they had never been in the pennant playoffs; they had never hosted a World Series in Chicago; and now, the Reds were coming to town with their best pitcher, Stuben Mitchell, rested, fit, and ready to add victory 27 to his 26–7 record for the year. Four of Stuben's victories this year had been against the Cubs. The Cubs had not beaten him in the last 3 years. Everyone in Chicago looked forward to the game in two days, but privately, they all expected the inevitable. Stuben and the Reds would win. The Cubs would lose.

After the game, Fast Ball and Lefty walked together through the tunnel and into the visitors' dressing room.

"Nice game," said Fast Ball. "I wish I could've set the table better for you."

"They just got lucky on you early," said Lefty.

Fast Ball and Lefty both knew that luck had nothing to do with the Cards' three-run first.

Neither player said anything else as Fast Ball went to his locker to shower and change. Because there were two female reporters from major newspaper sports pages covering baseball this season, no reporters were allowed in the locker room after a game. The league had set up an interview room adjoining each locker room. The manager and a few players went to the interview room for thirty minutes after each game to provide reporters with quotes to use in their articles. Fast Ball had been interviewed countless times after victories and losses. One of his best career memories was the excitement of the interview room after the last of his five-career no-hitters just 4 years before.

Today, however, he was glad that he could hide from reporters by staying in the locker room. He worried about his friend and the criticism Russ probably would get for starting him today, but there was nothing he could say or do to help Russ now. Fast Ball did not go to the interview room. He knew that Russ would understand.

The team's plane back to Chicago was not scheduled to leave for two more hours due to a scheduling error with the airlines company. Unlike a few of the more financially successful teams, the Cubs did not own their own plane or airline charter service and had to rely on scheduling charter flights with small market airline companies. The occasional inconvenience was annoying, but charter flights, even late ones, still beat the worn-out buses that Russ and Fast Ball had ridden in the minor leagues as 18-year-old players.

As Fast Ball sat in front of his locker, some of the younger players were playing cards in one corner of the dressing room. A few of the veterans who had played in the junior circuit American League were watching the Yankees and Tigers on television. Those teams were involved in their own pennant race in the AL East. Everyone was very quiet.

Fast Ball closed his eyes and replayed the first inning in his mind. The location of all his pitches had been good. His control usually was not a problem, even as a young flame thrower. His velocity, however, had abandoned him in the last four weeks. His arm was both old and tired. With his curve ball not working, the Cardinals had been sitting on his fastball. Rethinking the start of the game with his eyes closed did not change the results. The Cardinals scored the same three runs in the first inning. When he opened his eyes, he saw Russ walking toward him. Fast Ball looked at the clock on the locker room wall and concluded that the interview time was over.

Russ walked straight up to Fast Ball and said, "Henry, I need to see you in the manager's office before I change for the flight."

There was distress in Russ's voice. Fast Ball was concerned that maybe his not going to the interview room had been a mistake. Maybe the reporters had blasted Russ for starting an aging veteran in the middle of a slump in such a big game. Perhaps he had over estimated Russ's understanding of his desire not to talk to reporters after the game.

Russ abruptly turned and walked toward the tiny office provided for the visiting team manager. Fast Ball followed. When they reached the office, Russ waited for the pitcher to go inside. After he did, Russ closed the door. That is not a good sign, thought Fast Ball.

"Henry," began Russ, "we play the Reds in two days in Chicago. Who do you think should pitch?"

Russ often asked his advice, and Fast Ball always told him exactly what he thought without regard to their different roles on the team. Russ was the manager, and Fast Ball always treated him with respect, especially in front of the other players, but behind closed doors, they were two old friends talking about a difficult decision.

"Well," said Fast Ball, "no one is pitching very good right now. Jules has a sore arm, but he's afraid to tell you. Willy is a left-hander, and the Reds are full of right-handed power. Carson pitched nine innings yesterday, and he won't be ready in two days. I'm your fourth starter, and I didn't throw that many pitches today, but you saw what happened out there. My arm is spent. You don't have any good choices."

"Henry," said Russ, "taking you out of the game was the second hardest decision I've made today. The hardest decision is that I'm going to release you and open up a roster spot for the playoff game. I'm bringing up Fred Farley to pitch against the Reds."

Fast Ball usually had been able to predict his friend's decisions, but he was not prepared for what Russ had just said. Fast Ball had been in the league long enough to know its bylaws. Being released and not being suited up and in the dugout for the last game of the season meant that he would not be eligible to compete in postseason play, even if the Cubs won the game in two days. He had just walked off the mound for the last time in his career. He wasn't mad. He was just stunned. He did not say anything. He just stared at Russ.

"I'll petition the league to let you rejoin the team and take Jules' place if we make the playoffs," said Russ. "That is, if I can get Jules to admit he's hurt. I'm sorry, Henry, but I think it's the best decision for the team under the circumstances. I hope you'll understand after you think about it."

Russ had always been a risktaker. In fact, that's how he hurt himself in spring training 17 years ago. He had been trying to score from first on a long single down the right field line when he barreled into the opposing catcher who had planted himself in front of home to block the plate. Fast Ball wondered if maybe Russ's penchant for risk had gotten the better of his judgment. Starting a Triple-A pitcher, even a supposed phenomenon like Fred Farley, in arguably the biggest game in Chicago's history was a huge gamble. If it paid off, Russ's place in Chicago baseball lore would be secure; if it didn't work, it could be the beginning of the end of Russ's dream to bring a division championship to the Chicago Cubs.

"Are you sure you want to do this?" asked Fast Ball, still in a daze.

"I don't want to do it, but my decision is final, Henry. I'm going to go shower. I'll tell Hooks and Tonic before I announce it to the rest of the team. I'm sorry."

Hooks Harrison was the club's best middle inning relief pitcher, and Tonic Tisdale was a power-hitting right fielder. Each had been with the team over 15 years. Hooks, Tonic, Fast Ball, and Russ had spent their entire careers in the Cubs' organization. All four men were close friends.

Fast Ball stayed in the manager's office for a long time after Russ left. When he finally checked the time, he saw that the flight back to Chicago was scheduled to leave in just one hour. He started to hurry because the team would be leaving for the airport soon. Then he realized that he did not want to fly back with the team. He decided that he would rent a car and drive back home. He might even call his wife, Madge, and ask her to meet him at the Lakeside Resort, where they had vacationed several years ago. As he thought about Madge, he realized how much he missed her that very minute.

When he walked out of the manager's office, he saw Hooks and Tonic. He could tell from their expressions that Russ had told them the news. The usual dressing room chatter suggested that no one but Hooks, Tonic, Russ, and Fast Ball knew yet what Russ had decided.

Hooks walked up to Fast Ball and wanted to hug him, but years of being a jock in an all-male environment kept him from following his natural instinct. He settled for a pat on the shoulder. Tonic followed with a shrug.

Fast Ball told them about his decision to rent a car and drive back to Chicago. They both immediately said they wanted to go with him. Fast Ball initially declined, but then said he would like for them to come along, if Russ said it was OK.

At first, Russ thought it would be disruptive for the team if all three players missed the flight, but then he realized his friend might need company. The trip home would only be about 250 miles. It might take them five or six hours, but the big game was two days away. Hooks and Tonic would be well rested by then. Russ knew that the companionship might be important for Fast Ball, so he agreed that Hooks and Tonic could miss the team flight and drive back with Fast Ball. After he thought about it, Russ wished that he could go with them, but his place was with the team. He also needed to tell the other players soon about releasing Fast Ball and calling up Fred Farley from the minors. He had already called Turk McGhee long distance to ask him to get Fred to Chicago early the next day. Russ said good-bye to Fast Ball, Tonic, and Hooks, then he and the team left for the airport.

Chapter 2

AFTER RUSS AND THE TEAM left, the locker room was quiet. There were four decks of cards scattered on the two round tables in the corner of the dressing area. Shuffles Wampler, the visiting team locker room attendant, silently went about his business of picking up wet towels and placing them in a large clothes hamper on wheels. Shuffles might have wondered why Fast Ball, Tonic, and Hooks were left behind, but he did not ask any questions. He had worked with the Cardinals for as long as Fast Ball could remember. He had a ready smile, but he never initiated discussion with the opposing team's players. Fast Ball always spoke to Shuffles and called him by name, but at that moment, he realized how little he knew about him in spite of the amount of time he had spent in his presence. Fast Ball reached into his pocket and pulled out a $20 bill that he pressed into Shuffles' hand as he, Hooks, and Tonic walked out the locker room door.

They could hear the cleanup crew in the stands picking up hot-dog wrappers and paper cups. Occasionally, one of the children of the crew members would stomp a paper cup at the correct angle, making a loud popping noise that reverberated in the vacant stadium.

As the three players made their way out of the visiting club's locker room, the locker room smells of tough skin spray and liniment were replaced by the scent of stale popcorn and spilled cokes.

No one said anything, because from experience, each knew where the closest taxi stand and rental car agency were located. As younger players traveling with their wives, they had occasionally rented a van to sight-see in the area around the stadium hotel during off days before a weekend series. Those days seemed long ago now, and they were.

The game crowd was almost completely gone, and there were only two cabs waiting at the right field cabstand. They took the first cab in line. It was driven by a smiling, dark-skinned driver.

Tonic told the driver their destination, and the three players climbed into the backseat. Hooks had shorter legs than either Fast Ball or Tonic, so he sat in the middle. The windows of the cab were down, and the air was humid. The players said nothing as they rode to the car rental agency. Hooks paid and tipped the cabdriver while Tonic made arrangements for the rental car. He selected a large, 4-door Lincoln big enough to be comfortable on the trip, and the three left the car rental agency. There was a complementary map folded on the front seat. Tonic was driving. He had acquired his nickname as a younger player when the guys would go out late after night games on the road. He did not drink alcohol but accompanied the other players as the designated driver. In the bars, he would order a tonic and water while he listened to his friends talk and waited for them to be ready to let him drive them back to the hotel.

It was almost 6:00. The charter plane was scheduled to leave at 6:10. Fast Ball wondered if Russ had told the rest of the team that he had been released. He wondered what their reaction had been. For some strange reason, he wondered whether he would be able to get and keep both his road and home uniforms. That seemed to him to be an odd thought, but it had been an odd day.

The three friends were quiet. Each was thinking about the events of the day, but they were also preoccupied with thoughts about their past years playing together for the Cubs.

The silence had not been broken since they left the rental agency until Hooks said, "Do you remember those two Lawrence, Louisiana, kids that were drafted 5 years ago out of the same high school program?"

"You mean the pitcher and catcher?" asked Tonic, already knowing the answer. "Of course," he added.

Hooks started again, saying, "I'll never forget the time Hank Story told them the first night of spring training that they had to let the air out of the tires of Deep Pocket's new Mercedes in order to be accepted by the older players."

Hooks continued, "Remember how Hank told Deep Pockets (which is what the players affectionately called the Cubs' current owner, Les Paul) and the parking lot security guard, Guns McGhee, what was up. Those two Louisiana boys, bless their hearts, were wide-eyed and eager to please. I honestly think they would have jumped off the top of the hotel in Orlando in hang gliders if a veteran player had told them it was necessary to be part of the team," he laughed.

The three friends recalled how the two young players had dressed in black, like they were going to poach alligators in a Louisiana bayou as they drove straight to the spring training camp lot where Deep Pockets had his car parked. Hooks slowly described how the two boys sneaked up on the owner's car like cats sneaking up on a bird feeder while Hooks, Tonic, Fast Ball, and half the pitching staff watched from Deep Pockets' Winnebago parked twenty yards away. Tonic and Fast Ball had heard their friend tell this story countless times, but they somehow never grew tired of hearing it again.

"I remember how bright the floodlights were," said Tonic.

"Bright," said Hooks, "does not do it justice. Just as those boys had three of the four tires deflated, it looked like the sun itself had decided to pay a surprise visit to the parking lot—accompanied by several asteroids and comets in the form of twenty-five Florida State Trooper police cars equipped with spotlights."

Fast Ball knew that it had only been four Florida troopers in two cars equipped with the usual sirens, flashing lights, and spotlights, but it probably did seem like at least twenty-five policemen to Willy and Bobby, the Louisiana high school graduates who were now pitching and catching, respectively, for the Okmulgee Cubs with the franchise's Double-A farm club in Oklahoma.

"When those fellas got up off the asphalt, it looked like Bobby had for sure peed in his britches and Willy looked as white as his shirt was black. Then when Deep Pockets came out of the Winnebago waiving his arms like he always does, I thought those boys both might die on the spot! I've never heard so many 'yes sirs' and 'no sirs' in all my life as they were trying to explain what they were doing there."

Fast Ball and Tonic were both laughing just as they had laughed inside the Winnebago 2 years ago. In fact, Fast Ball was laughing so hard he cried. It felt good to laugh and cry at the same time with his friends.

As he wiped the tears away from his eyes with his left hand, Fast Ball looked at his watch and saw that it was almost 7:00. The charter flight would be landing soon and Madge would be expecting him home by 8:00. He wanted to call her so she wouldn't worry. He asked Tonic to pull off the service highway and look for a pay phone and a place to eat. Tonic took exit 26 and drove toward a small town 2 miles off the main highway. The three had learned years ago that small-town cafes off the beaten track usually had better food and friendlier service than highway restaurants. As they were approaching downtown, all three saw something that caught their attention. They looked together at the unmistakable lights of a baseball park at the edge of the small town.

Fast Ball had often expressed his belief that people are attracted to television not so much by content as by the lights and colors of the tube. He believed that the story is incidental; the lights are what attract. He called his idea the Moth Theory of Medium. These local baseball park night lights in the distance were more powerful to the three players than a TV to an 8-year-old. They looked at each other. Tonic said, "Why not?" and pulled off the paved road into a dirt parking lot. He parked next to an old stepside Chevy pickup truck like the one he'd had as a high school senior in Florida. Pausing briefly, he admired the smooth lines of the fender skirts for a few seconds before catching up to Fast Ball and Hooks, who were already headed toward the concession stand. Over the crackling public address system, Fast Ball could hear the words of the Little-League Pledge:

> I TRUST IN GOD.
> I LOVE MY COUNTRY
> AND WILL RESPECT ITS LAWS.
> I WILL PLAY FAIR
> AND STRIVE TO WIN.
> BUT WIN OR LOSE,
> I WILL ALWAYS
> DO MY BEST.

Fast Ball had memorized those words as a 12-year-old before a regional all-star game and had never forgotten them. He had taught them to his daughter and son. He silently wondered when someone would file a lawsuit asking the U.S. Supreme Court to ban the pledge from the game.

There must have been almost 200 people at the game scattered in lawn chairs, on blankets, and in the stands. Crepe paper in red and white adorned the rails of the third-base stands. Green and gold ribbons and balloons laced the first-base dugout and stands. *This must be some type of playoff game,* he thought.

As Fast Ball took two deep breaths, his sense of smell gained control over his sense of sight. The smell of hot dogs caused his stomach to growl. In spite of everything that had happened over the last six hours, he was hungry.

"Chili and cheese or plain?" asked Hooks.

"One of each," said Fast Ball.

"Me, too," added Tonic.

The mustard for the hot dogs was in yellow squeeze jars that they could wrap their hands around instead of in the large pump buckets like those found in major-league stadiums. The men behind the food counter all wore tall hats with some type of crest printed on the front. They smiled when they took Hooks' order.

14

Hooks and Fast Ball got cokes. Tonic ordered a 7-Up. Fast Ball stood behind Tonic, who was bigger than he was, hoping that he would not be recognized. Most of the fans in the Chicago area would recognize Hooks and Tonic, but they were not quite as well known outside of Chicago. Even the most casual fan, however, recognized Fast Ball. This was both a blessing and a curse that Fast Ball had accepted. Tonight it was a curse that he wanted to avoid. He walked a few steps away from the concession stand and watched the players as the team in the third-base dugout took the field to the sound of hoots and hollers.

The trio picked up their hot dogs and drinks. Tonic grabbed a handful of napkins. Together, they walked down the left field line where they spotted a large, circular, concrete base at the bottom of one of the left field light standards in foul territory. The concrete support provided a perfect bench and an inconspicuous place for them to sit, eat, and watch the game.

The first batter hit a long line drive between the left fielder and center fielder that rolled all the way to the chain-link fence just below a used car dealership sign. The leadoff double brought back painful memories of that afternoon. Fast Ball was able to escape his thoughts about the Cubs' game and refocus on the game at hand when the next batter, Lacy Shawn, was announced over the still-crackling public address system.

Lacy was also his daughter's name, and as he squinted through the low-light conditions of the dimly lit field, he could see long, blonde hair stringing out behind the next batter's batting helmet as she stepped into the batter's box.

Women reporters in the interview room . . . girls playing little-league baseball . . . he thought to himself. Fast Ball had grown up in a conservative town at a time when men and women occupied traditional roles. At first, he had resisted cooperation with female reporters and had scoffed at the idea of a lady umpire when he had heard about one in the minor leagues. But having a daughter had changed all that.

As a child, one of the most important things in his life was playing pickup baseball games before and after school, peddling his bike to Little-League practice on the weekends, and going with his dad to some of the local high school games, especially when they played semipro teams touring from the oil refinery plant in Pasadena, Texas.

He wanted his daughter, Lacy, and his son, Jason, to have the same opportunity to learn about baseball, both as a player and as a fan. That realization as a parent had made him one of the team leaders in granting equal access to female reporters during press day gatherings.

The batter, Lacy Shawn, took the first pitch for a called strike. She then swung and fouled off three of the next six pitches before working the count full. Lacy checked her swing on the next pitch, which was called a ball. She tossed her bat back towards her dugout and ran full speed to first with her long hair trailing behind her. Runners were on first and second with nobody out, setting up force plays at second and third. The infield fly rule would be in effect.

"Nice at bat," said Hooks.

There they sat . . . three grown men with an aggregate annual salary of over four million dollars . . . watching a Little-League baseball game in a small town on a cool night in October, having just eaten slightly over $6 worth of hot dogs sold by smiling men in funny hats.

Fast Ball, Hooks, and Tonic were caught up in the emotion of the noisy crowd and cheering players as they watched the first innings before leaving with the score 5 to 3 in favor of the Red Birds (the red and white team) over the Bears (the green and gold team).

"I'll take the next shift," said Fast Ball as they walked to the rental car. "You guys need to rest up for the big game."

Hooks hopped into the passenger side front seat and Tonic stretched his long legs in the backseat as Fast Ball started the Lincoln and drove out of the dirt parking lot and back toward the highway. It was just after 8:00.

Soon, Hooks reached over and flipped on the radio. "Let's see who won the Yankee game," he said. He quickly switched through a half dozen channels before he realized that the same voice was on each channel. Hooks stopped punching the radio channel buttons, and the three friends listened as the announcer said:

"Repeating this hour's top story, the Chicago Cubs baseball team is circling Chicago's O'Hare Airport with a defective landing gear that won't come down. Spokesmen from O'Hare Airport have told the media that they are preparing runway number 2 for an emergency landing by covering the runway with a highly lubricated foam designed for such situations. The Cubs, who lost a 4–0 game today to the St. Louis Cardinals with veteran pitcher Henry 'Fast Ball' Harvey taking the loss, are scheduled to play the Cincinnati Reds in two days in a one-game playoff for the National League East championship and the right to play for the National League Pennant."

As the players strained to listen for further details, Fast Ball remembered he had forgotten to call his wife to tell her that he was driving home with Tonic and Hooks. Fast Ball looked for a highway exit as the radio commentator continued his description of the circling aircraft and the need to consume fuel before attempting to land in order to reduce the threat of fire and explosion. He spotted a flashing sign that said "Jake's Sports Bar and Grill." Quickly, he pulled into a new asphalt parking lot.

Chapter 3

RUSS, THE COACHES, THE EQUIPMENT manager, the trainer, and the team left Fast Ball, Tonic, and Hooks behind in the Cardinal's locker room as they made their way out the main rear door and into the waiting bus to go to the airport. The mood of the team was still subdued because of the loss, but Russ was glad to notice that a few of the younger players were beginning to laugh quietly and make a joke or two as they boarded the bus. Russ was a serious, demanding manager, but he did not discourage camaraderie and practical jokes because he felt it was important to keep the team loose and having fun. So long as the players listened when he and the coaches were teaching and explaining techniques and strategies, and so long as the team members played with focus, he wanted them to have fun and be themselves with each other and with him.

No one was carrying any luggage. That was another advantage of the major leagues over the minor leagues. As a manager in the minor leagues, Russ had helped load the bats, balls, towels, dirty uniforms, and everything else before leaving a park for the drive to the next stadium. With the Cubs, the equipment manager and his crew took care of all those details including, thankfully, washing the dirty uniforms.

A few of the players carried portable radios or tape players with ear phones. No loud music on buses or airplanes was one of Russ's few rules. Russ carried his briefcase. It contained his seemingly endless pages of player information and statistics. He rarely went anywhere without his briefcase. Most of the managers in the league used statistics occasionally to make decisions before and during games, but the older managers primarily managed on instinct and personal experience. Russ knew that instinct and hunches were a valid part of coaching, but he usually made decisions during a game based on data taking into account every conceivable type of baseball statistic.

He updated his information on all teams in the National League daily through the use of a sophisticated scouting report system under which the paid scouts for the Cubs filed weekly reports about each game played in the National League. These reports were sent to the Cubs' main office in Chicago every Monday. The reports contained a myriad of details about each game and its players using a data sheet designed by Russ. A full-time statistician in Chicago received the weekly reports and generated a central data file that was then shipped to Russ every Tuesday. Russ would review the new information and update his records each week. Master copies were maintained at the team's Chicago office.

He was not self-conscious about consulting his briefcase records during a crucial situation in a game. These habits had resulted in his being called "The Professor" by some sports writers and announcers. It was a title to which he did not object, because he wanted to be known as a serious student and teacher of the game. He knew that he wasn't brilliant; he was just thorough and methodical in his preparation for his job. He was sure his system worked. He just hoped it would work for one more game.

He and Shorty, the first-base coach, always sat next to each other on return flights to Chicago. During flights home, Russ made out the lineup for the next game and then slept on it before making it final. He often asked Shorty for his thoughts after he had made up his own mind. He and Shorty always sat in adjacent aisle seats at the front of the plane. The seat next to each of them stayed vacant on all flights.

After Shorty and Russ had taken their seats and watched the players file past them, he thought he could tell that some of them had noticed the absence of Fast Ball, Tonic, and Hooks. Dickens Farley, the bullpen catcher, had even stopped to tell Russ that the three men had been left behind at the stadium. "I know," said Russ, "I'll explain in a minute."

Russ knew he had to announce what he had done before taking off for Chicago. He had not decided exactly what to say, but he decided it should be short and to the point. He was good with numbers and statistics, but he had never been very comfortable with words. That was a disadvantage because managers had a great deal of media responsibility. Over time, however, he had become better at interviews and speeches. His first step toward being comfortable had come in Mexico not long after his career-ending injury while he was coaching for the Monterrey Tigres. Russ had taken 3 years of high school Spanish and, although he was not fluent, he could make his way through lunch, travel, and baseball practice communicating in Spanish for himself and the U.S. players, most of whom couldn't speak Spanish at all.

The Monterrey Tigres' manager, Sparky Tuft, couldn't speak a lick of Spanish. Some people proclaimed Sparky didn't speak much English either. Russ drew the assignment of handling interviews for Sparky, and he got to be pretty good at it. He figured that if he could wade through interviews and postgame shows in Mexico in his broken Spanish, he could certainly do it in the U.S. in English. He was wishing that he could explain to the team what he had just done in Spanish as he stood up to address the squad before the plane left the terminal.

"As some of you have noticed," he said, "Fast Ball, Tonic, and Hooks are not on the plane. This afternoon, I decided to release Fast Ball and bring up Fred Farley from our Triple-A club to join our pitching staff for the next game. Tonic and Hooks are driving back to Chicago with Henry, rather than flying back with us.

"Henry is disappointed at being released, but he understands the decision and why I think it is best for the team and our chance to win the division.

"We will have a practice tomorrow at the usual time to go over a few things for the game in two days."

When he sat down, it seemed to him that it was extremely quiet in the cabin. He was glad to hear the jet engines roar and drown out the silence as the plane started toward the runway. He settled into his seat and glanced at Shorty, who had known about his decision before they started for the airport. He had trouble reading Shorty's reaction to the whole idea. Based on past experience, he knew that might mean disapproval.

He reached over into the empty seat next to him and grabbed his briefcase. The pages of data were his security blanket. He began to work on his starting lineup for the playoff game. The plane braked for the pilots' last-minute checks before takeoff and the engines were put in full forward thrust. With a slight jerk, it gathered speed down the runway and seconds later, they were airborne, headed for Chicago and a showdown in two days with the Reds.

Russ combed his records and reviewed every team member's lifetime batting average against Stuben Mitchell. He explored different offensive and defensive combinations. Halfway through the flight, he finished preparing his starting lineup except for the pitching position. Satisfied, he passed it across the aisle to Shorty.

Shorty nodded his approval and handed the proposed lineup back to Russ. Shorty rarely made lineup change suggestions to Russ. Russ had noted with interest that most of the time when Shorty did make a proposed correction, it was for a player that Russ had inserted because of a hunch. This time, Russ was going completely by the book.

He looked at his watch. It was almost 6:30. They would be landing soon. He had noticed the slight decrease in air speed as they slowly reached the apex of their flight. Then he closed his eyes and fell asleep.

At first he thought the tapping on his shoulder was a dream. But when he opened his eyes, he saw a stewardess bending over him. "The captain would like to see you," she said. In his years of flying, he had frequently been asked by the pilots or flight crew for baseballs autographed by the team or by particular players. It was part of the territory, and he always obliged.

This time, however, he was mildly irritated that he had been awakened for such a request so late in the flight. The stewardess opened the cockpit door and Russ stepped in. He did not see a baseball or baseball cards in either the pilot's or co-pilot's hands. The words from the pilot caused his blood to run cold. The landing gear was stuck and unable to be extended properly. He heard all the options and was advised they would be circling the airport for at least an hour and a half while consuming fuel and continuing to run through backup procedures.

"I thought I'd tell you first," said the pilot, "to see if you wanted to tell the team before I did."

"No," said Russ, "I'm the manager on the ground. You're in charge up here."

As he walked back to his seat, the pilot began his clinical explanation of the problem over the intercom. He had a good voice, thought Russ, and he was glad to have noticed that the pilot also had grey hair. Russ was hoping that meant he had experience in the type of emergency landing they were about to undertake.

After the pilot finished his comments, the stewardess began a detailed explanation of landing procedures, including how to sit, how to open the emergency doors, and how to deploy the CO_2-activated emergency door slides for quick departure from the plane. Then Russ stood up and began to walk down the aisle. He could feel himself coaching again. He did not like speeches, but he felt comfortable in small groups or in one-on-one conversations. He quietly reassured each player. As he was approaching the tail of the plane, he noticed that there seemed to be more players than usual in the back part of the cabin. He guessed that everyone had seen the same newspaper pictures he'd seen of plane crashes. The tail section was almost always intact.

Having taken care of his self-defined responsibilities, he returned to the front of the plane. Now his thoughts were dominated by his wife, June, and his two kids, Tucker and Alana. He hoped he would see them and hug them soon. As he sat down across from Shorty, he noticed that Shorty was reading an article in *Sports Illustrated* about the Yankees and Tigers series. Nothing ever bothered Shorty. That was an important reason Russ had asked Shorty to stay on as a coach after he had taken over the team last year.

Almost ninety minutes later, he heard the click of the intercom button and the pilot announced, "Crew, prepare for emergency landing. Passengers, prepare for final descent."

Somehow, the words "final descent" didn't sound too promising. He saw Shorty put down the *Sports Illustrated* and reach for a *Sports Afield*. It was very quiet on the plane. He noticed that the plane's carpet was blue with white flecks as he placed his head between his knees while the plane lost altitude. It had been a long day.

Chapter 4

MADGE HARVEY HAD MADE CHICKEN spaghetti as her contribution to the potluck dinner at June Freeman's house. Madge, June, Wallis (Hook's wife), Sylvia (Tonic's wife), and several of the other players' wives and kids watched many of the out-of-town games together at the large home theater room that was adjacent to the swimming pool in the backyard of the Freemans' house. When Russ had agreed to accept the Cubs' managerial job (as if there had been any doubt), the only thing he tried hard to negotiate with Deep Pockets was a signing bonus big enough to build a large rear-projection TV screen video room next to his cabana and backyard swimming pool. Russ was a hard worker, and he recognized the necessity to prepare for games by watching films of both his players and opposing players, especially pitchers. But he did not want to spend all of his nongame working time at the stadium's projection room. Russ wanted to be able to work at home so he could have some quality time with his wife and kids during the season.

Deep Pockets, a devoted family man himself, had agreed to the bonus. In addition, he had made arrangements with the stadium contractor and his personal homebuilder not only to add a large theater room, but also to build a putting green, wet bar, and lawn bowling court. The existing cabana was enlarged and a covered porch was added for a Ping-Pong table. Even though Deep Pockets did not own the most successful franchise in the league from either a financial or a competitive standpoint, when he made up his mind to do something, he did it first class. The end result was both a perfect place for Russ and his coaches to meet in an informal atmosphere for late-night work sessions and a logical gathering spot for the players' wives and kids to watch the games and eat when the players were out of town.

No one had eaten much of Madge's spaghetti or the other food dishes after today's game with the Cardinals. The older women, in particular, had the same sense of dread that gripped all the baseball fans in Chicago. The Cubs had come close before, only to lose the division to other teams in the last week or two of the regular season. Madge knew that Henry's chances to be a division winner and to have an opportunity to play in a World Series had come down to one game.

She was sad. The other women were also, but they made an extra attempt to cheer up Madge by staying to visit long after the game had ended.

The young children had eaten most of the deserts and devoured the homemade ice cream that June had made in the Freemans' industrial-size electric ice-cream maker. Today's flavor was blueberry. The young kids were spending their seemingly limitless supply of energy in the pool while Tucker and Lacy stood watch. Tucker Freeman and Lacy Harvey were the 19-year-old son and 17-year-old daughter of Madge and June, respectively. Tucker's and Lacy's willingness to stay around and watch the younger kids swim was driven by their being responsible young adults, but their growing feelings for each other also played a role. Besides, they both took their dads' careers seriously and had not felt much like going to the Chicago Alley Bowling Lanes with the other older children who had left the house a little over an hour ago.

Almost all of the wives were still at June's house when Madge looked at her watch and decided it was time to leave. Fast Ball would be home soon, and she needed to take the extra casserole dish of chicken spaghetti that she'd made earlier in the day out of the refrigerator and put it into the oven. She left the video room and went into the kitchen to get some of the salad she had put aside for her husband. The other women were also preparing to leave when the phone rang. June answered it.

"Mom!" It was the voice of her 17-year-old daughter, Alana. June could tell that Alana was upset. She immediately worried that Alana had been in a wreck while driving the other kids from the bowling alley in the family's van.

"Mom," she said again. This time June could tell for certain that she was crying.

"What's wrong? Are you all right?"

"I'm OK," she said, "but the plane carrying Dad back to Chicago is having difficulty landing." Alana told her the information being reported over the air. June told Alana to drive home, but to be very careful. After hanging up, she walked quickly to the media room.

"Listen, everybody," she announced as she punched on the big screen TV where she saw a side view of a commercial airplane descending from the clouds. All the wives stopped their packing and listened to the newscast. There was a sign in the bottom right-hand corner of the screen that said *"Live, Special Bulletin."* The young kids could be heard laughing in the pool next to the cabana while the tearful women held hands and watched the screen.

Chapter 5

FAST BALL, HOOKS, AND TONIC were watching the same scene along with over 400 patrons at the grand opening of Jake McDonnell's 28th location of a national franchise called Jake's Sports Bar and Grill. By combining big-screen TVs, good food, a bowling, pool, bar, shuffleboard, indoor lawn bowling, and a free throw shooting area at a single venue, Jake McDonald had managed to prosper. Millions of other Americans were watching the same TV picture on every major network. The drama had begun unfolding during rush-hour traffic radio bulletins on the West Coast, and now, virtually everyone in the sports world was watching during evening prime time. A presidential debate was scheduled for later in the evening, so several TV sets were turned on in expectation of witnessing more mudslinging in what had already been a spirited campaign. Instead, the viewers found a drama of a different sort.

The opening night crowd at Jake's would ordinarily have been loud and active, but all friendly competition in the various amusement games had stopped while everyone quietly watched the silhouetted plane make its approach to a foam-covered runway guarded at one end by waiting fire engines and ambulances. It seemed strange to hear Red Trickey, one of baseball's best play-by-play announcers (and the voice of the

Chicago Cubs), describe the action instead of hearing a familiar evening anchor.

The largest TV in the bar was televising the landing attempt using split screen viewing. One angle was from overhead the airplane, and Fast Ball assumed it must have been shot from a traffic helicopter. The other angle was level with the runway with the plane approaching from the left side of the screen. It seemed to Fast Ball that the overhead shot showed the plane coming in slightly off the center line of the runway, but it was hard to tell exactly what was happening.

The ground level screen showed the back half of the plane hitting the runway foam first. The contact with the runway resulted in a shower of white foam that looked like a giant motorboat rooster tail on the calm surface of a lake. The subsequent contact of the plane's belly with the runway caused the plane's wings to shudder visibly. Now that the plane had touched down, Fast Ball could see definitely from the overhead shot that it was not traveling in a line defined by the middle of the runway.

As the plane lost speed, the pilot tried to lightly touch down the front of the plane where the main landing gear should have been hanging down, but it was clear that he was having difficulty keeping the plane's wingtips parallel to the sides of the runway. The left wing dipped faster than the right wing until the left wing and front bottom of the plane hit the surface at almost the exact same instant. Unfortunately, the left wing hit the grass infield adjacent to the runway while the fuselage of the plane slid across the specially prepared runway.

The friction difference caused by the wing scraping grass while the belly and rear of the plane scooted along the foamed runway eventually caused the right side of the plane to swerve forward and rotate to the left until the plane was, for all practical purposes, going sideways down the runway. At that point, the efforts of man were only marginally influencing the outcome of the landing attempt. The laws of physics and whatever divine intervention prayer could muster were in control of the results.

The plane never flipped, nor did it rotate on the ground a full 360 degrees. By the time it came to rest, however, it was impossible to tell which way it had been flying originally from the angle it occupied at the end of the runway. The right wing was broken at the wing's intersection with the body of the plane. The left wing pointed skyward at almost a 45-degree angle.

Circling the airport to use fuel had reduced the possibility of fire according to Red Trickey's flawless description of the action, but everyone watched in horror as smoke began rising from the tail section of the plane.

There were over 15 fire engines parked on both sides of the runway close to where the plane had come to rest. In a well-synchronized plan, the fire trucks were speeding toward the smoking plane in singular lines like the spokes of a bicycle wheel with the doomed plane at the hub. The larger trucks with tanks full of a nontoxic foam were within fifty yards of the plane when the fire causing the smoke became visible to the millions of television viewers. The lead trucks were followed by smaller trucks and ambulances. Sirens were not turned on, but lights were flashing everywhere. Descending darkness added problems to the rescue efforts, but runway lights and spot lights were aiding visibility.

There were four exits to the plane. One was in the rear, which was of no use because of the fire. Two were just behind each wing on different sides of the aircraft. The remaining exit was the regular entrance door just behind the cockpit.

The exit behind the left wing flew open and the TV screen abandoned the split screen approach to show a full shot from the traffic helicopter hovering overhead. A carbon dioxide-propelled escape slide shot out of the door. Because the left wing was angled up instead of parallel to the ground, as would normally be the case with the plane at full rest on its wheels, the end of the rescue slide also angled skyward. The end of the slide was at least 15 feet off the ground even though the weight of the slide and the flexibility of its material worked with gravity to bend the slide in a half-moon arc extending from the body of the plane toward the ground.

That exit was of no use to the doomed plane's occupants.

The exit on the right wing side of the plane was opened next. The TV camera shifted to ground level. The ground camera was closer than the one overhead, and the camera was of better quality. With a close-up shot, everyone watching television could see the gas-operated slide eject. Because the right side of the plane was tilted down, the rescue slide did not fully extend and jammed against the runway blocking the exit. Two hands could be seen in a desperate attempt to push the slide out of the doorway.

The airport fire captain's truck was the lead truck on the left side of the plane. It had combined forces with four other large trucks to douse the fire at the rear of the plane. Smoke, however, continued to pour out from the tail section and out from a crack in the fuselage a third of the way from the tail toward the left wing. The airport's fire captain, who himself had been a pilot before a mysterious vertigo problem grounded him 3 years ago, saw the problem that had developed with the exit slide on the left side of the plane's midsection. He tilted the automatic hook and ladder on his truck toward the left middle exit by using the control lever inside the fire engine cab. He placed the end of the fire truck's sturdy ladder perfectly against the side of the plane at the opening of the left central exit. He told his co-driver to maintain that position while two other members of his truck's crew began helping passengers down the ladder to safety. There was still a threat of explosion, but the fire seemed to be under control.

The fire team captain jumped to the ground and ran toward an equally large fire truck adjacent to the front left exit behind the cockpit. He saw the door open. No slide emerged, probably because the plane's pilot recognized the futility of trying to use the emergency slide due to the angle of the plane to the ground. Through a combination of words and pointing, the fire captain explained the need to the other truck's driver to imitate the rescue ladder effort of the truck he had just left. Quickly a ladder was locked into place at the front exit. Just as quickly, some of the players and crew members began emerging from the front door.

On the right side of the plane an emergency vehicle equipped with mechanical jaws ripped chunks from the inoperable slide and cleared an opening on the right emergency exit. Because of the closeness of the right exit to the ground, that exit proved to be an efficient one for the plane's passengers to use.

Meanwhile, the fire trucks continued to pour white foam over the outside of the plane. Everyone emerging was showered in white. Some of them were bloody; some were limping; some were being carried in the manner of a player hurt on the field.

The players' wives watched through their tears. They were still holding on to each other. The young children were no longer in the pool. Everyone was in the media room watching the scene unfold. The older children had returned from the bowling alley in time to watch the plane come to rest. Some of the camera angles made it possible to recognize faces and there were shouts each time a specific player was recognized, but no one became too excited about single successes. They were in this together and only complete safety for all the passengers could be celebrated to the fullest.

As organized as the rescue effort was, the scene was still one of chaos. Red Trickey's description on the Chicago station being watched by the wives was sprinkled with names of the players as they emerged from the plane. He never mentioned Fast Ball, Hooks, or Tonic. Madge, Wallis, and Sylvia had not seen their husbands' faces. There was no mention of the fact that those three players weren't on the plane because no one participating in the news coverage knew that Fast Ball had been released and that he had decided to drive home with Tonic and Hooks for company. Madge, Wallis, and Sylvia continued to watch the screen, anxiously looking for their husbands.

Miles away, Fast Ball had seen enough. "We've got to get home," he said as he walked toward the sports bar door. Hooks and Tonic followed him because they did not know what else to do.

As they were about to exit from the front door, they heard someone yell, "Fast Ball, Hooks, Tonic, what are you doing here?" When they turned around, they saw Hank Terwilliger, a former major-league relief pitcher.

Hank had been one of baseball's best closers, having almost 20 years of service with five different teams in both the American and National League before his retirement from the Los Angeles Dodgers last year. The fact that his head was completely bald and that he had a red handlebar mustache as wide as the antlers on a South Texas deer made him one of the most recognized faces in the world of sports. Hank had been with the Cubs for almost 3 years during the early part of his career. He and Fast Ball had stayed in touch over the years.

"I'm not sure what I'm doing here or even what I'm doing," said Fast Ball, still in a daze from the television scenes of the last thirty minutes. "I'm just wondering how I'm gonna get out of here and back to Chicago. What are you doing here?" he asked in a reflex response to his old friend's question.

"Jake asked me to sit in for an autograph session after your game today."

Fast Ball knew Hank was referring to Jake McDaniel, the owner of the Jake's Sports Bar & Grill chain. One of the unique features to Jake's bars and restaurants was that they included retail space with a sports memorabilia store that sold everything from autographed baseball bats to major-league batting helmets and baseball cards. This multiproduct marketing was one of the keys to Jake's success. Young patrons could go into the card and memorabilia store and stay outside the drinking part of the building while the bar patrons could easily wander in from the interior entrance and buy hats and other souvenirs to take to the televised games in the primary viewing room. Asking current or retired players to attend specific games or events for autograph sessions cost money, but the publicity and extra sales that popular, well-known sports heroes generated was good for business. Fast Ball had helped Jake open two of his new locations on opening nights in Texas last year during postseason play. Jake always attended the opening night of a new franchise location.

By not having to look at the drama still unfolding on TV inside the bar, Fast Ball was beginning to think again . . . opening night . . . Jake's Sports Bar & Grill . . .

"Hank," asked Fast Ball, "is Jake here?"

"Yea, he's back in the office with Boots."

Boots was Jake's combination bodyguard-chauffeur-accountant. Boots was big, mean, friendly, and smart . . . all at the same time.

"How did he get here?" asked Fast Ball.

"The usual," said Hank.

"The usual" meant that Jake had flown into a local airport in his Learjet. Jake had been a pilot in the navy, and after he became rich, he bought the fastest and biggest corporate jet he could find. To him, it was not a status symbol, it was love. Jake loved speed and flying almost as much as he loved making money.

"Let's go talk to him," said Fast Ball.

The four men walked back into the building. All of the TVs were still on the same channel. Fast Ball tried not to look, but it was impossible not to glance at the big-screen TV on the north wall. There was no fire visible. That was good. There were several ambulances around the plane. That was bad. Red Trickey's voice could be heard to say that ambulances were delivering the injured to at least three hospitals in the vicinity of the airport in order not to overwhelm the emergency room of the closest hospital. There were no known fatalities at this time, but not all of the Cubs' players were accounted for due, in part, to the fact that several hospitals and different ambulance services were involved in the rescue effort.

The men walked to the upstairs office and knocked on the door. Boots opened it after recognizing Hank's voice. The office was small with a large, one-way window overlooking the bar and restaurant's main room. When the door closed, it was much quieter in the office, but Fast Ball could still hear Red Trickey's inescapable voice describing the scene of chaos at the Chicago airport. The light in the office was brighter than in the bar.

Jake had been watching a wall-mounted TV behind his desk with his back to the door. When he turned around, his mouth opened wide and for maybe the first time in his life, he was utterly speechless. He shut his mouth, and opened it again. This time words came out.

"Fast Ball, Hooks, Tonic," he recited the players' names. Big-time sports was his business, and he knew all three of the baseball players by name, just as he knew the major players in professional football, basketball, and hockey by sight. He made name recognition and familiarity with players part of his business.

"I don't go to church as much as I should, but I've been praying hard tonight. Looks like some of my prayers have just been answered. How did you get here?" he asked, as if he truly suspected divine intervention.

Hooks and Tonic let Fast Ball do the talking as he quickly told Jake about being released, renting a car, and being joined by Hooks and Tonic for the drive to Chicago. Everyone was still distracted by the sights and sounds coming from the TV behind Jake's desk.

"Jake," said Fast Ball at the end of his comments, "I need a favor."

"I know," said Jake, "let's go."

Then he added, "Give Boots the keys to your rental car. Get your luggage if you have any, and meet me at the white van out back."

"Boots, give their car keys to Harlan and tell him to take care of the details on the car return."

Then he looked at Fast Ball, stood up, and shook Fast Ball's hand real hard. "This is great," he said. "Ten minutes ago, I was feeling lousy. Now, I can do something to help. I've got to go downstairs to the card shop before I leave. See you out back. Hank, you can come, too, if you want." He dashed out the door. Jake is a man of action, thought Fast Ball.

The players weren't sure how fast Jake's jet plane would fly on the way to Chicago, but they didn't see how it could go much faster than the van Boots was driving to the local airport. He drove faster than any CPA they had ever known.

Boots radioed ahead to the airport to notify the pilot to have the plane ready with a flight plan filed for Chicago.

"Do you want to listen to the radio?" asked Boots.

The three players looked at each other. Their facial expressions said no. In the excitement, it had not yet occurred to the players that their wives thought they were on the plane.

It was almost 9:15 p.m. when Jake's plane took off, veered to the left, climbed, and leveled off at cruising speed, headed for Chicago. Flying gave all of them, except Jake, an uneasy feeling given the affairs of the day. But being able to actually see Jake at the controls and knowing how organized he was in his daily life gave each passenger a sense of well-being. It was not long before they were descending below the cloud cover and toward one of the runways at Chicago's airport. Through the distance, they could see the irregular flash of bright spotlights and blinking lights competing with the usual runway lights in straight rows. They were glad to feel the plane's wheels touch the runway.

Chapter 6

AT JUNE FREEMAN'S HOUSE, 14 of the players' wives, along with 26 of their children ranging in age from 19 down to six months, were still huddled in a contiguous mass in front of the media room's large TV. Darkness had descended on Chicago long ago, but the television picture was still bright and clear due to the emergency vehicle floodlights and airport spotlights in coordination with high-resolution cameras.

Many passengers had either walked, or been carried, from the plane's three working exits, but no one at the house, or on TV, had an exact count. The women were alarmed when a close-up shot through a telephoto lens showed three men wearing gas masks and asbestos fire suits entering the right middle door to the plane. Madge wondered if the authorities knew there were still passengers unaccounted for, or if they were just trying to be thorough in their rescue effort.

No one had seen Fast Ball, Tonic, or Hooks come out of the plane. Madge knew that they would have been sitting close to each other, as was their custom on flights. She, Sylvia, and Wallis were growing visibly more concerned with each passing minute of uncertainty.

Under June Freeman's direction, two of the women had contacted the three area hospitals where news reports had indicated the injured were being taken for treatment. Slowly, they were compiling a written list of the players' locations and general conditions. There were several broken bones, a few minor burns and assorted cuts and bruises, but there were no known casualties. There were, however, three names still missing from the list.

Russ, June had learned, was at Chicago Hospital about 20 miles from the Freeman's house. She had seen him being carried from the front exit by a fireman who used a safety harness to keep from falling off the extended ladder. Russ had been one of the last passengers to exit, just before a uniformed man that she assumed was a pilot. She noticed that Russ's removal was a slow process. To her relief, she saw him talking to the rescuer, and he did not appear to be bleeding. She was anxious to leave for the hospital and to see him, but she did not want to rush Madge, Sylvia, and Wallis. They were still glued to the TV, waiting for the men wearing gas masks to emerge.

Some of the women had started leaving for the hospitals where their husbands had been taken. It was agreed that the older children would stay at the Freeman's and try to put the younger kids to sleep using the multiple sleeping bags in the cabana available for that purpose. June had called two professional babysitters from her church to help with that project. They were scheduled to arrive in a few minutes.

Before long, it was just June, Madge, Sylvia, and Wallis left with the children and the constant companionship of the TV. June had switched the channel earlier to ABC because a hospital switchboard operator had told one of the wives that they were sending the names of the rescued passengers to ABC's local news affiliate for broadcast purposes. Fast Ball's, Hooks', and Tonic's names had not appeared in the subscript messages at the bottom of the screen.

"Why don't we go to the hospital and ask Russ about them?" June said gently. "He was one of the last people to leave the plane, and I'm sure he wouldn't have left unless he knew they were safe."

Madge decided that there was no use in continuing to watch the news coverage. There were still no complete, reliable injury reports available. She had seen the three masked men crawl from the plane empty-handed. All of the objective clues were positive, but she could not understand why there was no trace of Fast Ball, Hooks, or Tonic. Madge agreed with June that the four of them should go to the hospital where Russ had been admitted.

Before leaving, Madge walked into the cabana room that had been expanded by Deep Pocket's contribution to the remodeling project to say good-bye to her son, Jason. He was helping the youngsters prepare for bed while keeping one eye on the small TV in the pool room, listening for news about his father. As she approached, she noticed how much he looked like Fast Ball when she had first met him at a high school dance over 25 years ago.

"I'm going to Chicago Hospital with June to check on Russ. While I'm there, I'm sure I'll see your dad. He'll be OK. Try not to worry."

Jason did not say anything, but he hugged his mom for a long time before she left. "Say hi to Dad," he said, trying to be as positive as possible.   In an attempt to be light-hearted, he said, "and tell him he still owes me $5 on our golf bet."

Madge left the pool room and joined the other women. June was driving in her car. She pulled through the circular drive in front of the house, turned left, and started toward the hospital. The radio was not on when the car was started. Nor did June reach over to turn it on for the latest news reports. No one suggested listening to it on the way to the hospital. In fact, very little was said during their drive. The quiet comfort of the car was a welcome contrast to the loud chaos of the last three hours.

June found a spot on the third floor of the hospital's parking garage adjacent to the hospital's main entrance. The four women took an elevator down to the first floor of the garage and walked under a covered walkway, through automatic sliding glass doors, and into the hospital. They stepped across a linoleum floor and stopped by a yellow sign that said, "Caution, Wet Floor." The hospital air was dry and smelled like the cleaning fluid used to mop floors. There was a slight floral odor from the flower and gift shop to their right. Each woman was familiar with the hospital from past visits. Some of those visits were happy and marked by births; others were sad and punctuated by illness, surgery, and even death. June was wondering how this visit would be remembered as they walked together to the front desk.

"I'm looking for Russ Freeman who was just admitted as a patient. Can you tell me what room he's in?" said June to the somber receptionist. The receptionist consulted her records. The wait was longer than expected as the receptionist continued her search.

Finally, she said, "He just left the emergency room and has been assigned to room 242." She did not look at the women as she talked. She stared straight at her desk's top records.

Madge asked, "Would you please see if you show a Henry Harvey as a patient. He should also be a new admission."

There was no sign of name recognition on the worker's face as she studied her sheets again. After repeating her earlier efforts, she looked up and said, "He's not listed." This time she looked at the women. There were no records to read on her desk. Sylvia and Wallis went through the same procedure regarding Hooks and Tonic and received the same negative response.

Madge said, "Let's go see Russ." She was shifting her concern about Fast Ball to her friend's need to go see Russ and reassure herself about his well-being.

There was a crowd surrounding the elevator bank, so the women walked toward the stairwell and climbed the single tier of steps to the second floor. When they walked into the hallway, they saw two women and one man, all wearing white, behind a desk to the right. They also saw signs indicating that rooms 201–230 were to the left. Rooms 231–250 were to the right. They turned right.

As they headed past the desk, the man who was the nurse in charge, said, "I'm sorry, but if you're going to a room, only two people can go in at a time."

The women looked at each other and Sylvia said to June, "Why don't you and Madge go in? Wallis and I will wait here." She pointed toward six chairs and a wooden bench lining the wall across from the nurses' station.

"We'll be right back," said June, "and tell you what he says about Hooks and Tonic."

June and Madge walked briskly toward Russ's room while Sylvia and Wallis sat down with a sigh. When the two women reached 242, the door was closed. June opened it quietly and walked in first. Madge was right behind.

Russ had his eyes closed. His left leg was elevated at a 20-degree angle and was outside the sheets on top of the bed. The raised leg was wrapped in an inflatable, temporary cast. June could see the leg cast and a few cuts on his left arm, but there were no other visible injuries. The women were wearing tennis shoes so their steps made no sound as they entered the room.

June walked around the bed and stood next to her husband. Madge stayed behind, just inside the door to the room. Russ opened his eyes as June touched his right hand.

"Hi," he said weakly, but with a smile. "I was wondering when you'd get here."

"I can't believe this whole thing," June said. "It was awful watching it on TV. I'm glad you're alive."

"Me, too," said Russ.

"Looks like you've been skiing," said June.

"I wish," he laughed quietly.

At that moment, Russ saw Madge out of the corner of his eye. His initial thoughts turned to Fast Ball and the game earlier that day. Even though he believed releasing Fast Ball to be the best decision for the team's chance to make the pennant playoffs, he still had an uneasy feeling that he had betrayed his longtime friend.

Out of a sense of guilt he said, "I'm sorry about Fast Ball." Russ was referring, of course, to his release of Fast Ball from the team. It did not occur to him that Madge did not know that Fast Ball had not been on the plane when it crash-landed. His words sent a chill down the spines of both women. *What had happened? Was Fast Ball hurt seriously? Was he dead?* It did not seem possible. But nothing had been happening according to plan during the improbable events of the day.

Just a few yards outside room 242 and in front of the nurses' station, Tonic and Hooks were hugging and kissing their wives while Fast Ball smiled. The male nurse did not recognize the players or understand their jubilation. "Please try to be quiet. This is a hospital," he said, as if the players and their wives would somehow be in awe of that revelation.

"Let's go to 242," said Sylvia to Fast Ball. "Madge is in there with Russ and June."

There had been no time to explain any of the details of their drive in the rental car to Sylvia and Wallis. Nor did the women care about details. At that moment, they only knew that Russ, Tonic, Hooks, and Fast Ball were alive and safe. They all wanted to celebrate their good fortune together, so they walked quickly toward Russ's room.

"Only two at a time," said the male nurse frantically. "Those are the rules."

Tonic said, "I tell you what. We'll go in there two at a time until we're all in there at the same time." Sylvia tried to reassure the nurse by saying they'd be out soon.

When they arrived at the door, Sylvia and Wallis went in first, shoulder to shoulder through the narrow door. They were smiling broadly. Their arrival coincided with Russ's remark to Madge about being sorry about Fast Ball. June and Madge looked at their friends, Sylvia and Wallis. Their smiles seemed out of place on the heels of Russ's comment. Madge was about to react to her friends' untimely smiles when she saw Tonic's face rising above Sylvia's head. Next, she saw Hooks, and then she realized the reason for her friends' happiness. She felt relieved for them, but she still had the ache of uncertainty about Fast Ball. That ache lasted for only two more seconds until she saw her husband. She rushed into his arms. She could make no sense out of Russ's statement about being sorry about Fast Ball, but it made no difference now. She was intermittently laughing and crying, as were the other women. It felt good to laugh and cry at the same time with friends.

Over the next ten minutes, there was a confused exchange of information about the crash, injuries sustained, why Hooks, Fast Ball, and Tonic had not been on the plane, and related items. Meanwhile, the male nurse had not given up on his mission to enforce the hospital rules. He barged into the cramped room. This time he was accompanied by an armed security guard. The guard, a life-long Cubs fan, immediately recognized Fast Ball, Russ, Tonic, and Hooks. Before long, he was asking for Fast Ball's autograph while he told Russ that he had just inquired through the security desk about the crash victims and been told that there were no fatalities or injuries beyond broken bones, smoke inhalation, and a few minor burns and bruises. Under the circumstances, that was good news. This exchange of information was taking place to the deep consternation of the male nurse.

"People, please," he said, "I have rules to enforce. I don't care if you're Roger Morris or Joe Domingo," he added with mistaken references to former baseball greats. "Rules are rules."

"We'll leave in a few minutes," Fast Ball told the security guard as he handed him a fistful of autographs on the hospital room stationery.

"They'll leave in a few minutes," the guard told the nurse. Exasperated, the nurse left the room. The guard soon followed, promising Russ that he would make inquiries to the security forces at the two other area hospitals that were accepting crash victims to determine the extent of injuries to the other players and coaches. As the guard left clutching his prize autographs, the phone rang.

June answered. Her side of the conversation included a brief description of Russ's injuries, a "yes," a "thank you," and an "OK" before she hung up. "That was Deep Pockets," she said. "He said he was late for a conference call but that he needs to meet with you at 8:00 sharp tomorrow morning. He'll come here."

"If he can get by that nurse," laughed Hooks.

"We'd better go," said Madge.

"Us, too," added the others.

"You need to get some rest," said Fast Ball to Russ as they all left, couples arm in arm, leaving June and Russ to share their happiness privately.

Chapter 7

THE NEXT DAY STARTED EARLY for Russ at the hospital. Two orthopedic surgeons, one from the hospital along with the team's regular physician, Dr. John Kirby, visited with Russ at 6:00. He had a hairline fracture of his left tibia. There was no swelling, and they were scheduled to replace the inflatable cast with a permanent one at 2:00 that day. It would be a walking cast. He also had multiple contusions and lacerations on his left arm and side. The pain in his lower back was of concern and x-rays would be required. Dr. Kirby suspected only bruises, but wanted to rule out internal injuries through a series of tests. If the tests proved negative, Russ might be released tomorrow morning, but not before.

Russ asked Dr. Kirby about the remaining players and coaches. "Remarkably, there were no fatalities," said Dr. Kirby. "You are my first visit today, so I'll know more later. I can tell you," he added, "that Legs Cooper broke his left arm. It's a clean break according to the x-rays I've seen, so he should be ready for spring training next year."

"I'll get with you this afternoon," he added, as he and the hospital surgeon left room 242.

Not long after their departure, the security guard from the day before dropped by.

"I called my contacts at the other hospitals and here's a list of the admissions and preliminary diagnoses of every coach and player for the Cubs," he said proudly as he handed Russ three alphabetized lists of names from the three separate hospitals treating crash victims. "The Chicago PD shows no fatalities."

Russ glanced at the list and was surprised at its detail. He thanked the guard as he put the list to one side, planning to review it more carefully later.

At that moment, the floor nurse assigned to Russ's room for the morning shift came in bearing needles and thermometers. She announced that she was there to take his temperature and a blood sample. She looked contemptuously at the security guard. Russ thought she must have heard a full report from the male nurse on the prior shift.

"Before you go," said Russ to the guard, "leave me a card. I appreciate your help. When we make the playoffs, I'll get you a couple of seats behind the dugout."

"Thanks," said the guard, beaming as he handed Russ a business card and walked out of the room with a happy lilt to his step.

After having his temperature taken and being stuck by the nurse, he was told that he would be given breakfast in five minutes. The clock on the wall said 7:30. He was wondering if Dr. Kirby might authorize his early release as he pondered what the nurse on the next shift might be like.

Breakfast consisted of a banana, bowl of cereal, orange juice, and glass of milk. It was close to the same breakfast he would have eaten had he been home. June called and said she'd be by at 9:30 with the kids. When he hung up, he looked again at the clock. He noticed it was almost 8:00 as the door flew open and in walked Deep Pockets and Peter O'Malley, the commissioner of baseball.

Commissioner O'Malley was one of the few commissioners of professional baseball who had never played the game at any professional level. His background was in advertising. He had handled the accounts of many of the country's largest manufacturers, automakers, and beer distributors before being asked to accept a pay cut to become the commissioner of baseball at $200,000 a year. He had agreed to accept the job if he could also get 5 percent of any increased television revenue that he was able to generate over the multimillion dollar contract with ABC that was scheduled to expire six months after he was to take office.

Because the TV contract that was scheduled to expire had been the biggest ever due to the increasing popularity of professional football, and because all analysts were predicting a financial disaster in baseball due to decreasing television revenues coupled with rising players' salaries, the baseball owners saw no downside in agreeing to the 5 percent demand. They also thought that Mr. O'Malley might be able to use his advertising background to enhance baseball's flagging image. Sadly, baseball was no longer considered by many to be America's pastime.

The owners, to their surprise and joy, had significantly underestimated Peter O'Malley's negotiating skills. Within four months from taking the job, he held a press conference announcing the largest TV contract by far in the history of not just baseball, but in the history of professional sports. He was flanked by the executives of two major airlines, one domestic and one foreign car company, two oil companies, and the world's largest beer maker and distributor. They were all only too happy to describe their alliance and sponsorship commitment to baseball for the next 6 years. Commissioner O'Malley's 5 percent of the increased revenue over the last TV contract amounted to nine million dollars a year for 6 years. At the same press conference, the commissioner announced that he was donating his regular salary to a baseball scholarship foundation organized to award college scholarships to ex-players drafted out of high school who had never made it as successful pro players.

Commissioner O'Malley could be a very charming man when he had time to relax and be himself, but he also had a reputation for being abrupt and to the point in his business discussions. Today, he was in a hurry.

After the obligatory condolences and comments, Commissioner O'Malley said, "Russ, the TV contracts for the postseason are all set in concrete. There is no way to change the schedule of the games due to conflicts with pro football and already-paid advertising commitments. The AL Pennant playoffs are scheduled to begin in three days. The NL playoffs are set in four days. Your winner-take-all makeup game with the Reds was originally scheduled tomorrow, and I am going to have to keep you on that schedule. Under the broad authority granted to me as the commissioner of baseball, I have also decided to waive the limit on minor-league players you can add to your roster to replace injured players for the playoff game up to a maximum of 30 active players. Do you understand my decision?"

"Yes," said Russ.

Deep Pockets knew it was useless to request any more consideration. The TV money had been the Cubs' financial salvation as a lower division team. There was no way to alter the scheduled games beyond what the commissioner had already agreed.

"Good luck," said the commissioner as he excused himself and walked out of the room.

After he left and before saying anything further to Deep Pockets, Russ picked up the phone next to his bed and dialed the Cubs' home office. True to form, the Cubs' longtime receptionist, secretary, administrative assistant, team cheerleader, and Mother Confessor to the players, Henrietta Moore, answered the phone. "Cubs. We're still here."

"Henrietta," said Russ.

"Hi, Russ. I thought you were dead." She recognized his voice as she did virtually every voice on the other end of the phone line.

"Henrietta, let me tell you what I need."

"Shoot," she said.

"I'm in room 242 at Chicago Hospital. As soon as you can have it delivered, I need the backup data book complete with our full roster statistics in the usual format. I want every piece of information we have about the active players on our farm teams."

"It'll be there within two hours," she said. "Take care of yourself."

Russ knew he could count on her as he hung up the phone. He then reached over and picked up the list that the security guard had left with him.

"Pull up a chair," he said to Deep Pockets. "Let's see what we got."

Russ was back at work. Deep Pockets could see that he had made a wise choice in hiring Russ for the long-term future of the franchise. He sat next to Russ so he could see the papers Russ was holding. Deep Pockets never meddled in coaching decisions, but Russ sincerely wanted his input, especially today. It was, after all, his team, thought Russ. Russ quickly told Deep Pockets how he got the list, and the two men began reviewing the injuries together.

After a brief visit with his wife and kids, Russ and Deep Pockets resumed their review of the injury list. They also compared the security guard's printouts with the list that June had compiled, based on her phone discussions with players' wives. There were no differences between the two sources.

In his usual organized fashion, Russ broke the lists down into three categories: (1) players who were not hurt at all, (2) players who were so seriously hurt that they could not play, and (3) players who were hurt but could possibly play. He knew that he would have to verify his information before making final choices, but he did not want to take time now to do that. He decided to make preliminary decisions based on the information at hand.

Just as he and Deep Pockets had finished separating the list into the three categories, Clark Sweeny, a delivery person from the Cubs' front office, walked in with the backup data sheets Russ had requested. Russ looked at the clock. It had been just less than two hours since he talked to Henrietta.

He grabbed the data book and went to work by listing the original starting lineup that he and Shorty had agreed upon in the plane. Then he compared it to the injury list categories. He concluded that the original starting shortstop, catcher, center fielder and second baseman could not play because of injuries. There is an old baseball maxim that good defense should be strong up the middle. From a statistical standpoint, losing his defensive strength in the middle positions was not good.

To make it worse, the backup players on the team roster in those same positions were also unable to play. After preliminarily reviewing his options to play some of the healthy players out of their regular positions, Russ shifted his attention to the farm club information. He reviewed the statistics, both offensive and defensive, for all players in Double-A and Triple-A. He paid particular attention to batting averages against right-handed pitching such as the Reds' scheduled starter, Stuben Mitchell. He noted that a few of the minor-league players had even batted against Stuben Mitchell before he made it to the big leagues.

Deep Pockets patiently watched and made occasional comments as Russ reviewed his records and wrote out a starting lineup. Finally, without explanation, Russ reached for the emergency call button pinned to his pillow.

Within seconds, a different nurse burst into the room. At first, Russ thought maybe there had been some mistake because this one was smiling. She was also very attractive and several years younger than the nurses on the prior shifts.

"What can I do to help?" she said.

"Can you access typing and Xerox equipment in the hospital's business office?" he asked.

She seemed puzzled, but responded, "Yes. Why?"

"I need a favor. Can you take this list and type it? I'll need five copies."

"Sure, why not."

Fifteen minutes later, she returned with Russ's lunch in one hand and the requested copies in the other.

Russ grabbed an apple off the lunch plate and began reviewing the typed sheets. He handed a copy to Deep Pockets. "Thanks," Russ said to the young nurse. She was still smiling. She had apparently not had enough experience with unruly patients in her brief career to be disenchanted with her job.

"You're welcome." She turned and headed toward the door. "By the way, my uncle is the pitching coach for the Reds."

Deep Pockets and Russ almost broke their necks as their heads shot up and they looked up at her as she opened the door. She turned and looked at them; she was still smiling.

"Just kidding," she winked. "Good luck," she added as she left the room.

"Remind me to hire her when the season's over," said Deep Pockets as he and Russ recovered from their distraction and began reviewing the proposed starting lineup against the Reds. Here are the players they saw as they gazed at the printed lineup:

Leading off and playing center field was Wheels Wilson. He was currently playing Double-A in Tennessee. He probably would have been playing Triple-A this year, but a spring training injury had limited his playing time early in the season. This was his second year in pro ball, having been drafted out of college where he was an Academic All-American as well as a second-string All-American player on the AP poll his senior year for the Miami Hurricanes. In spite of being smart and good, his best-known characteristic was speed. The old-timer scouts in the Cubs organization talked about Wheels and Cool Papa Bell in the same breath. Cool Papa Bell, it was said, was so fast that when he flipped the light switch in his hotel room at night, he could climb into bed and get under the covers before the light went out!

Batting second and playing left field was Pat Smith. He was one of Russ's veteran players, having been in the league almost 10 years. Five of those years had been spent with the Cubs. He was also fast and could hit with occasional power.

Batting third was Guns Gleaton, the Cubs regular third baseman. The medical reports showed that his left knee was sore from the crash, but Russ knew that Guns had been playing with a sore left knee most of his career. Third base did not require that much range. It was primarily a reflex position, so unless he was really hurt, he should be able to play. Russ would have to verify his status before game time. Guns batted right, so he would still be able to push off his right leg.

Batting cleanup was his regular right fielder, Tonic Tisdale. Tonic was leading the team in RBIs (runs batted in) and home runs. Russ was glad that he had agreed to let Tonic drive home with Fast Ball and Hooks.

Batting fifth was his second-string first baseman, Mark Yudof. The starting first baseman, Albert Gomez, had a broken leg and concussion. Mark Yudof had been the first baseman for 6 years before losing his starting position to Albert Gomez in spring training this year. Russ had thought about moving his second-string right fielder to first, but had decided that Mark's experience at the position would be a plus. It would be important to balance the inexperience of the minor-league players in the lineup with the experience of the veterans.

Batting sixth was Pudge Jones, the Triple-A catcher who had caught every ball pitched by Fred Farley this year. It was a huge loss not having Legs behind the plate, but Russ liked the idea of having a pitcher and catcher who were familiar with each other. They were both very young and Russ had hoped to bring them along more slowly, but the circumstances required accelerating the process.

Batting seventh was the shortstop, Scooter Stanford, from Triple-A, followed by Tiny Martin, another Triple-A rookie, playing second base. Scooter and Tiny had led their Triple-A league in double plays this year. Russ decided it would be better to treat them as a unit rather than playing his more experienced infielders out of position. The pitcher, Fred Farley, would be batting ninth.

He flirted briefly with changing the starting pitcher to Bob Carson, who would now have an extra day's rest, but he decided against it. He stayed with his initial choice of Fred Farley, but he still wanted to talk to Fred before making the final decision.

51

If he put this team on the field to start the game tomorrow, he would be playing 4 veterans and 5 minor-league players (counting the pitcher.)

"Why don't you take the lineup sheets to the other coaches and see what they think," he said to Deep Pockets. "Be sure to ask Shorty to call me. Also, if you could, please ask Henrietta to contact all the minor-league players on our roster of 30 and tell them to be at the stadium by 9:00 tomorrow morning."

Deep Pockets took the lists and instructions, and with the enthusiasm of a messenger boy on his first assignment, he dashed out of the room. He also took the security guard's injury lists so he would know where to have the lineup copies delivered. Russ thought how lucky he was to have an owner that he liked and who was so gracious and thoughtful toward his players and coaches. He also thought how lucky he was to be alive after the crash.

No sooner had Deep Pockets left the room than Turk McGhee and Fred Farley walked in together. Turk was first. He wore khaki pants, black tennis shoes, and a Chicago Cubs T-shirt. He carried a Cubs baseball cap in his hands. The top of his bald head was white in contrast to his tan forearms. He was one of the most polite men Russ had ever met. Russ thought it peculiar that someone so nice had "Turk" as a first name. Turk carried himself as if he were about to ask Russ for permission to marry his daughter.

Towering above him and wearing cowboy boots, blue jeans, and a western shirt with a prickly pear-shaped bolo tie was Fred Farley. Maybe it was because he was lying down, but it seemed to Russ that Fred had to bend down in order not to hit his head on the door frame as he walked into the room. It also seemed as if Fred had to angle his head sideways as he walked through the door so as not to hit his enormous handlebar mustache on the sides of the doorjamb. He was carrying a black cowboy hat with a cactus design hat band that matched his tie. And he was much bigger than Russ had remembered.

"We just saw Deep Pockets, and he said to come on in. I hope we didn't wake you," said Turk.

"Not at all. I was hoping that Henrietta had reached you and asked you to come to the hospital. As you can see, they won't let me walk to the stadium today."

Fred just stood there not knowing whether to smile or to act sorrowful. He reached toward the bed and offered his large, calloused hand to Russ. "Nice to meet you again. Thanks for asking me to pitch."

"Do you think you're ready?" Russ opted for the direct approach.

"Give me the ball and I'll stick it in the catcher's mitt so often that the umpire will lose his voice calling strikes." There was no hesitation in Fred's response. Turk watched with the pride of a new father.

Russ pressed the emergency call button on his pillow again. In walked the same pretty young nurse who had helped him with the lineup sheets.

She eyed Fred with what appeared to be equal parts of fear, curiosity, and admiration. She was about half his size, but then so was almost everyone else in the world.

Earlier, Russ had scribbled out the Reds' usual starting lineup. He handed the list to the nurse along with some other statistics about the Reds' players. "I need three copies of these sheets. Be sure to copy the tendency sheets under the header 'How to Pitch.'"

"Got it," she said. "But I'll have to make four copies. Need one for my uncle, you know." She winked again at Russ as she bounced out of the room.

In fifteen minutes she was back with the requested documents. Russ looked at them and thanked her. She was still smiling. It looked as if she were trying to mentally measure Fred's mustache as she left the room back first. Fred seemed to be measuring her, too.

"Turk, go to the stadium and get the film file. Go over each Reds' hitter with Fred using these tendency sheets. Spend two hours on it today and two hours in the morning. Then follow your usual routine that you developed at the Triple-A club.

"See you tomorrow," he said to Fred.

"I'll be ready," affirmed Fred as he and Turk walked out.

Turk walked out last, turned, and gave Russ the thumbs-up sign. Russ looked at the clock. It was almost 2:00 p.m.

As soon as Turk and Fred walked out, in walked the hospital's orthopedic surgeon. *The next time I stay here, thought Russ, I'll ask them to put a revolving door in my room.*

"It's time to get your walking cast," announced the doctor.

Russ winced as he sat up. In the flurry of activity, he had not noticed the pain in his leg. He focused on it for the first time in a few hours. He was ready for the cast. It was his ticket out of the hospital and to tomorrow's game.

Chapter 8

IT WAS 7:00 A.M. THE NEXT day when the phone rang at Fast Ball's house. He was already one hour into his daily routine that began with stretching exercises and sit-ups. He could smell the aroma of the coffee percolating in the automatic coffee machine as he got up from the mat in his workout room to look for the portable phone in the den.

"Hello," he said as he picked up the receiver. It was not unusual for his friends to call him early because they knew he would be awake.

"Henry," Russ was at the other end of the line, "I figured you already knew, but I wanted to make it official. The commish never knew about the release, and he has allowed me to expand the roster to 30 anyway due to the crash. You're on the team for tonight's game."

"I figured as much, but it's nice to hear it firsthand. Am I starting?" he asked jokingly.

"No, but since you didn't pitch much the other day, you might see some action." Then he added, "I'm sorry about letting you go."

"Don't worry about it. Besides, the way things turned out, Somebody upstairs was looking out for me."

"There's a team meeting at 10:00 at the club house."

"Yeah, I heard."

"Be there. And, don't forget your Boy Scout knife." Click.

That was Russ's way of telling him to be prepared.

Russ really didn't have to tell Fast Ball to be prepared. He knew that Fast Ball was the most prepared player in the league. He began his preparation the day he turned pro and had never let up since. Exercise, the right food, and moderation in all things were Fast Ball's guiding mottos. He took a lot of ribbing for his clean living from some of the players, but deep down, they respected his dedication. More importantly, as Russ knew, many of the younger players imitated Fast Ball's lifestyle.

Fast Ball had worked up a sweat from the last of his fitness exercises before the phone rang. After hanging up from talking to Russ, he grabbed a towel from the bathroom linen closet and walked toward the kitchen, flipped on the light, poured his wife a cup of coffee, and took it to her in the bedroom. He did not drink coffee himself, but he liked the smell. He wrapped his hand around the top of the cup and funneled the aroma to his nostrils as he delivered his morning offering to Madge.

He knew that she was awake, although she pretended to be asleep as he walked into the bedroom. She opened one eye and looked at him as he sat on the edge of her side of the bed.

"Let me guess. That was Russ calling to say you're back on the team and penciled in as the starter tonight," she kidded, not knowing how close she was to being correct. "Two out of three. Not bad. It was Russ, and I am back on the team, but I'm not going to start."

"That's great," she said as she sat up. She had been concerned about Fast Ball's not being part of such a big game. She put her arms around him and said, "I'm glad you're OK."

"Me, too," he replied. "It all still feels like a dream. Being released, driving home, the plane crash, the hospital, the game."

"It does have an unreal quality, but I smell coffee, so we must be awake." She reached for the cup on the nightstand. Fast Ball kissed her lightly on the cheek as he got up from the bed.

"You know, I've got a good feeling about the game. I'm going to go see what the sports guys think about our chances," he remarked as he made his way toward the front door to get the newspaper.

Fast Ball ordinarily did not read articles about the Cubs' games at all, whether he was scheduled to pitch or not. The crash, however, had turned the playoff game into more than just a sporting event. In turn, he was more than just a player. He was a fan. He wanted to read everything in the paper about the game just like every other person in Chicago.

When he walked out the front door for the paper, he could see that the sun was beginning to peek above the horizon. The morning was calm. The air was cool and moist. As he bent down to get the paper, he could see dew glistening on top of the winter rye he had planted in the yard just three weeks ago on a Thursday travel day before a weekend series at home. When he removed the plastic cover from the morning paper, the headline shouted, "The World Waits. Cubs vs. Reds in NL Showdown."

Almost all of the front page was devoted to articles about the game and the aftermath of the airplane crash landing. There were pictures of the flight crew, a human interest story about the fire chief who headed the rescue effort, and interviews with players and coaches. It was a fairy tale in real life for every journalist. This is going to be a good paper to read, thought Fast Ball as he headed back to the house and to a breakfast of blueberry pancakes, fresh fruit, and milk.

At 8:15, the phone rang. It was Hooks.

"Well, it took a disaster, but I hear you're back on the team. At least nobody was killed."

"Not yet," said Fast Ball in mock anger.

"Say, Legs can't drive that fancy foreign car of his with one arm in a cast. I told him I'd pick him up for the meeting. Do you want to go earlier and catch the first act?"

"Sure, I'll be over by 8:30," said Fast Ball. The "first act" was a reference to the press conference that Russ always held at 9:00 a.m. on home game days. This one ought to really be something, and Fast Ball wanted to see it. After quickly finishing the article about the fire chief captain at the airport, he told Madge he'd be back after lunch, then he left for Hooks' house four blocks away.

When Hooks, Fast Ball, and Legs arrived at the stadium, they could not believe their eyes. It looked as if the game had already started because of the number of cars in the parking lot. TV sound trucks were everywhere. All the letters of the alphabet were represented on the sides of media cars, trucks, and vans.

The three players drove past the media members and fans and into the "players only" parking lot. Legs was very quiet. Fast Ball knew that he did not accept injury well, and Hooks had been trying to cheer him up since they first picked him up that morning. Fast Ball thought maybe his efforts had been successful when he looked in the backseat by way of the rearview mirror and saw Legs smiling.

With his good arm, Legs opened the door and almost sprinted toward the entrance of the players' lot. "Jamatsu," shouted Legs. At first, Fast Ball thought maybe Legs was delirious.

A Japanese man carrying cameras and video equipment that appeared to outweigh him by twenty pounds turned toward Legs and broke into a wide grin. He shoved his many cameras into the hands of a startled assistant and ran toward Legs. The two men shook hands vigorously.

Before joining the Cubs, Legs had played 1 year in Japan. Like many Americans, he had trouble adjusting to Japanese culture . . . that is, until he met Jamatsu Sakamora, Japan's most revered sports photo journalist.

Legs and Jamatsu became fast friends after Jamatsu had done a pictorial essay about Legs and the art of throwing out base runners trying to steal second base.

When Legs returned to the States after accepting the Cubs' offer, the only person he truly missed was Jamatsu. The two men corresponded on a regular basis, and Legs was happy when he heard Jamatsu was coming to the U.S. to cover the World Series.

Apparently the excitement and drama of the plane crash had triggered an early arrival.

Hooks and Fast Ball were glad to see Legs excited and happy. They excused themselves to attend the press conference while Legs and Jamatsu renewed their friendship. Fast Ball looked over his shoulder as he entered the players' entrance to the clubhouse and saw Jamatsu signing his name on Legs' cast.

When inside the clubhouse, Fast Ball could see that many of the other players had also arrived early, probably for the same reason. No one wanted to miss the press conference.

Out of the corner of his eye, Fast Ball saw Turk McGhee. Turk was famous among the Cubs as being one of the best developers of young pitchers in the minor leagues. Next to Turk, facing the other way, was a tall, broad-shouldered man being measured by the club's uniform attendant and tailor, Tape Measure Logan. Tape Measure looked exasperated.

"How am I going to have a uniform big enough ready by tonight?" he complained.

"You'll figure it out. You always do," said Fast Ball as he walked up to the scene.

At the sound of Fast Ball's voice, Fred Farley turned around and flashed a toothy grin. It was hard to notice that he was smiling because it was difficult not to focus solely on Fred's huge mustache.

"Still got the stash, I see."

"Yep," said Fred. "It hypnotizes the batters. Nice to see you."

"Are you nervous?" asked Fast Ball.

Fred looked around the locker room as if he were about to tell Fast Ball the location of the Lost Dutchman's Gold Mine. "A little," he said, "but don't tell any Reds."

Fred was cocky and had learned the art of intimidation. Tonight would be his supreme performance, thought Fast Ball.

"Tape Measure," Fast Ball told the tailor, "leave him lots of neck room so he can swallow his chicken bone early." He then turned to Turk. "Nice to see you. Take care of your star pupil here. You might want to get him to trim that stash a little for the interview room after the game."

Fast Ball turned and walked toward the press conference. As he walked into the side stage of the interview room, he was almost blinded by the camera lights. Through the glare, he could see dozens of microphones of different heights crowded next to each other on the table in front of Russ. Russ was just beginning his press conference, saying, "I've been told by the baseball commissioner that tonight's game might be delayed two hours because the bus chartered by the Reds to travel to Chicago is not able to make quite as good time as the plane they were originally scheduled to use."

The packed audience laughed at his tongue-in-cheek reference to the airplane crash. Russ continued. "Before opening it up for questions, I'd like to tell you about the minor-league players that have joined our roster for tonight's game." Russ proceeded to provide the writers and telecasters with samples of the detailed information that lived in his briefcase. He delivered an injury report about the regular players that lacked only x-rays. He then described the special roster for tonight's game based on the emergency rules adopted by the commissioner that allowed him to expand his roster to 30 players for the game. He pointed out that the commissioner was going to let all the injured players who were physically able to attend the game to sit in the Cubs' dugout.

He said he had not settled on a starting lineup (because he did not want to give the Reds extra time to prepare for specific players), but that it would include at least a few of the minor leaguers. The professor was delivering a thorough lecture, and by the time he was through, there were hardly any questions to be asked about the game or its players.

That didn't stop the barrage of wide-ranging inquiries. The early questions were about the crash landing itself. They were followed by questions about his cast and whether the injuries to some of the key players were career threatening. He was also asked if he thought more recovery time should be permitted to allow some of the veteran players with minor injuries to heal before the game was played.

Fast Ball enjoyed watching his friend's even-tempered, businesslike approach with the press. After the allotted hour, Russ rose, thanked those in attendance, and walked off the side stage where Fast Ball and a dozen other players were standing.

"Glad that's over," said Russ to Fast Ball and Hooks. "Let's get to work."

When Russ and the players in the interview room walked into the main clubhouse, this is what they saw: Five veteran players were sitting with casts either on their arms or legs; seven other veteran players were wearing bandages of one sort or another; fifteen veteran players looked more or less normal; two veteran players and two coaches were in wheel chairs; and eight minor-league players who had never been in a big league clubhouse preparing for a regular season game were standing around with bewildered expressions. Everyone was milling around in the same general area waiting for the team meeting.

"Listen up," said Russ, "we've got some things to talk about."

Everyone gathered around him. He stood on top of a bench in the large open area in front of the regular team members' lockers.

"Well," began Russ, "the circumstances of tonight's game are unique, to say the least. I just finished a press conference attended by over 300 reporters. I'm sure that if they were polled, there wouldn't be ten of them who would bet on us to win this evening's game. Most of you know me. Some of you are new to the team and know me only by reputation. All of you are aware that I place a great deal of emphasis on statistics and averages when making decisions. I have carefully examined the statistics of the probable starting lineups for both teams in tonight's game. On paper, our team, as newly arranged, has an even chance of winning. Whenever a game is statistically even, the outcome is often decided by preparation and desire.

"I know that everyone in here wants to win this game, not just for ourselves, but for every player who has ever worn a Cub uniform and for every Cub fan who has supported this franchise year in and year out.

"The Reds have won the division, the pennant, and the World Series before. They might be complacent. They surely will be overconfident.

"Preparation is the potentially deciding factor. All of you who have been with the team the entire year have been preparing for this game with me since spring training. Those of you who have just joined our team today have been prepared for a game like this by one of the best minor-league coaching staffs in organized baseball. The only thing missing is to finish our collective preparation today. Shorty, I want you and Turk to meet with all of the pitchers in conference room A and go over every player on the Reds' team using our hitting analysis notebook. Begin with their anticipated starting lineup, but go through their entire roster.

"Legs, I want you and Pudge Jones also to meet with the pitchers and go over the same information. Legs, you also need to tell Pudge everything you know about their players' base running capabilities. Also, get him used to your voice so he'll be able to pick it out tonight if you shout instructions to him from the dugout.

"Sam," he said addressing one of his other coaches, "I want you to take the outfielders to conference room B and use the hitting tendency printout for the Reds to discuss how you want to position the outfielders for each batter.

"Wilson," he addressed the infield coach, "I want you go to conference room C and go through the same exercise with the infielders. Scooter, you and Tiny need to be part of that meeting and go over who should cover second base depending on who is batting and who is running on first base.

"I want all of the injured players to participate in the meetings by position. Lunch will be brought to each room. There will be enough variety in the food choices for every appetite. While you eat, I want every player to say something to the group about the game, about the accident, about whatever you want to talk about. Get to know each other and tell each other why it is important to win. I don't want to hear any shouting. There will be plenty of time for that tonight after the game.

"At 1:00, we will meet here again. Those of you who have batted against Stuben Mitchell will receive a printout of every at bat you've ever had against him. When we break up this afternoon, study it. See the pattern. Visualize hitting his pitches squarely. Think about his past pitch selection against you.

"At 1:15, you'll be free to leave, to stay, to sleep, to do whatever you want to do to relax and prepare yourself to concentrate for tonight's game. Be back at 5:00 to dress, go through BP (batting practice), and play, coach, or encourage your teammates, depending on your role.

"Any questions?" Russ looked around the room.

It was very quiet. After a few seconds, Herman Liske, a reserve outfielder who was in a wheel chair, raised his hand. He was sitting next to Bobby Bexler, a utility infielder who was also in a wheel chair.

Herman asked, "Coach, when we win, can Bobby and I go to the pennant playoff in an air ambulance or will we have to take the regular team flight?"

There was laughter all around. As Russ surveyed the laughing players, some of whom knew each other and some of whom were strangers, he had an idea.

"Shorty," said Russ, "go see if you can find Flash Cube." Flash Cube had been one of the sports page photographers for the *Chicago Daily* newspaper for over 30 years. He had attended every Cubs game during that time except for half the games last season due to a serious illness.

"I want to get a picture of the team," said Russ.

Shorty left the room in search of Flash Cube. He knew just where to look, because most of the sports beat regulars lingered in the coffee room after morning press conferences to swap stories.

Legs, who was sitting close to Russ when he gave his instructions to Shorty, stood up and whispered a question to Russ.

"Sure," responded Russ to Legs, "I think we should do our part to enhance international relations."

Legs dashed off in search of Jamatsu.

Legs, Shorty, Jamatsu, and Flash Cube returned together two minutes later. Jamatsu was smiling broadly. Flash Cube looked appreciatively toward Russ. Both Jamatsu and Flash Cube were carrying large camera bags, tripods, and lens cases. It took a few minutes for the players and coaches to walk, hobble, or roll into position. There were so many of them that they had to stand (or sit as the case may be) very close to each other in order for the two photographers to get them all in the picture. After ten or so flashes each, the players and coaches went to their meetings. It was almost 10:45.

Jamatsu and Flash Cube agreed to go immediately to develop their shots in Flash Cube's traveling darkroom van in the parking lot. They also agreed to share all pictures with each other. Russ whispered something to Flash Cube and Jamatsu before the two photographers left. "No problem," said Flash Cube after looking to Jamatsu for approval.

When the two photographers left, Russ was alone. He could hear his irregular footsteps on the thin carpet as he slowly limped toward his office. He planned to review data about the Reds' hitters while the players and coaches were meeting.

It was simple to him. The teams were almost even. He believed the Cubs wanted to win more than the Reds. If everyone worked hard this afternoon, they would be prepared and as unified as possible. He had a plan. He was implementing his plan. He thought the plan would work.

At 12:50, a knock sounded on his office door. "Come in," he said.

There stood Jamatsu and Flash Cube holding sixty copies of an 18 by 10 photograph of the Cubs, with wheel chairs, casts, Band-Aids, and all. Underneath the photograph was a printed inscription that read "THE CRASH-LANDING CUBS, DIVISION CHAMPS."

"Thanks," said Russ. "This is perfect." He stood up and headed for the 1:00 meeting carrying the photos.

When Russ walked into the dressing room, the players and coaches were arriving from their respective meetings. Those in wheel chairs were being pushed by team members. Russ could overhear discussions among several players regarding pitching tendencies. Others were discussing outfield positioning. There were occasional laughs but no horseplay. The room had the sound of serious business tempered by quiet laughter. Russ liked what he saw and heard as he set the photographs facedown on a table next to the lockers.

When everyone had gathered, Russ asked for reports from each conference room meeting. The reports were given by the coaches and supplemented by a few of the veteran players. As the reports were presented, Russ noticed that all eyes were on the speakers. He also noticed that the players were occupying about half of the floor space that the team had filled in their first meeting that morning. At first he thought that maybe some of the players were missing, but then he realized that everyone was sitting closer together. He smiled to himself.

When the reports were concluded, Russ made a short speech built around his earlier theme of preparation. He told the players to return to the stadium in time for both infield practice and batting practice. The game was scheduled to begin at 8:10. He reminded the players that the crowd would be a sellout with fans arriving early. Deep Pockets had reserved the usual five suites in the Cubs' Hotel two blocks from the stadium for those players who wanted to relax within walking distance and avoid the hassle of driving to and from the ball field. He finished his remarks by handing out the photographs. As the players and coaches left the locker room, Russ felt satisfied that he had done all he could on such short notice. He felt good about the game because he believed everything he had told his players and staff. His comments about the odds of winning and the importance of preparation were not ploys to motivate his team. They were the statistical truth as he saw it.

As Russ made his way to his office, he noticed that his broken leg was aching. He decided to take two aspirin and lie down on the couch in his office. He looked at his watch before closing his eyes. It was almost 2:00. By 2:05, he was sound asleep.

Chapter 9

TWO BLOCKS AWAY, IN ROOM 207 of the Cubs' Hotel, Red Trickey was reviewing his notes for tonight's game. Red had been the radio announcer for the Cubs for 23 years. Since the hotel had been built, he had prepared for home games in room 207 in order to avoid traffic jams en route to the stadium.

Everyone in the Chicago listening area knew the sound of his voice even if they were just casual baseball fans. In addition to his local following, Red had developed a national reputation among sports fans and media executives. He had been offered numerous job opportunities to leave the Cubs' small market network and broadcast national games for both TV and radio. He had turned down all offers except for a syndicated weekly baseball show with ABC Radio in order to stay with the Cubs.

In addition to being a well-known, respected announcer for the Cubs, Red was a Cubs fan, and the thought of leaving his team was a thought of treason. When he was a young boy, he listened to Ronald Richey do the play-by-play for Cubs' games and he dreamed about being able to make his living the same way. To him, he had the perfect job, and no amount of money could lure him away from his seat for every Cubs' home game immediately behind home plate.

Even though his job was secure as long as he could talk and see, Red did not take his job for granted. In his mind, he had a solemn responsibility to be at his best every time the "On the Air" sign flashed in his announcer's booth.

The last two days had been extremely busy ones in preparing for the Cubs/Reds game. He had recorded interviews with the fire chief who had led the airport rescue effort and with the baseball commissioner. He also had recorded comments from the 3, 4, and 5 hitters in the Reds lineup as well as comments from his longtime friend, Deep Pockets, owner of the Cubs. He had wanted an interview with Fred Farley, but out of respect for Deep Pocket's request that the rookie not be bombarded by the media, he had refrained.

Red was trying to decide in what order he was going to use the prerecorded interviews in his pregame show scheduled to start at 7:30. After deciding on the sequence, he called the studio so they could arrange the tapes in the appropriate order. It was 3:00 when he hung up the phone. He then called the hotel's front desk to request a wake-up call at 4:30. He followed that by phoning his wife to ask her to call him at 4:35 as a backup precaution. Then he stretched out on top of the bedspread with his clothes on and shoes off.

As he lay there, he thought about all the years he had spent as a fan of the Cubs. He knew the importance of tonight's game to the franchise. He was nervous, not for himself, but for the team. He hoped they would play well. He closed his eyes and imagined what it would be like to win, play for the pennant, and go to the World Series. By 3:15, he was sound asleep.

Chapter 10

TWO HUNDRED MILES AWAY FROM the Cubs' stadium, Lloyd Stevens was finishing his afternoon chores on the family farm. As he drove his old, stepside pickup truck down the dirt road adjacent to his southern-most field inspecting the germination of the winter wheat planted twenty days ago, he saw a neighbor's family car en route to his house. Lloyd glanced at his watch and saw that it was almost 7:00. The pregame show would commence soon, and he pressed harder on the accelerator in order to speed up his trip home.

Lloyd and his wife of 35 years, Louise, had invited their neighbors to the house for the Cubs/Reds game.

One of Lloyd's prize possessions was an old battery-operated, vacuum tube RCA radio with a Morning Glory speaker that had been given to him by his grandmother over 35 years ago. With the gift came stories about how his granddad would invite the neighbors to the old homestead to listen to the broadcast of significant baseball games such as the World Series. In that day, the old pecan wood radio was one of the few radios in the county, and the only one with a large, Morning Glory speaker loud enough to be heard at a distance of almost twenty yards.

In his grandfather's time, the ritual of listening to an important game when baseball was the nation's pastime was often preceded by a sandlot game played by fathers and their sons while mothers and their daughters watched and laughed.

The world of farming was a lot more complicated now, with high-tech fertilizers and complex government regulations, than it was when his grandfather was alive. The world of baseball was a lot more complicated now, too.

Nevertheless, in Lloyd's mind, baseball had retained most of its purity from a simpler time, and he enjoyed recreating his grandfather's tradition by occasional parties to listen to big games. Tonight's game was the biggest game of all in Cubs' history, and he wanted to share the experience with his neighbors. Today, there would be no afternoon game among fathers and sons because it was a workday. Lloyd was excited.

His house was equipped with a new 24-inch color TV, and in a concession to modern technology, the picture would be on. But the centerpiece of the gathering would be his granddad's radio that still worked, although tonight, it would be supplemented by his wife's hi-fi radio, just to make sure that none of Red Trickey's play-by-play calls would be missed.

When Lloyd reached home, several of the neighbors had already arrived. He did not worry about being late, and he did not concern himself about wearing the dirt of a hard afternoon in the field on his clothes. He walked into his bathroom, scrubbed his hands hard with the sandpaper soap in the lavatory and then set about the business of properly welcoming his guests and setting up the old radio and new hi-fi radio for the evening's broadcast.

His wife busied herself in the kitchen with their daughter and her husband. When both radios were turned on, Lloyd could hear Red Trickey interviewing the airport fire chief, who was rapidly becoming a national folk hero. Even though the crash had taken place only two days ago, legends were emerging to take their place next to some of baseball's all-time great stories.

Some of the guests were seated at the dining room and kitchen tables. Others sat with legs crossed on the floor of Lloyd's living room, eating food from the kitchen buffet as the last pregame interview with Deep Pockets was being concluded. Lloyd looked at his watch and saw that it was almost 8:00. He rubbed his freshly scrubbed hands together in gleeful anticipation of the game to follow.

At precisely 8:00, after a commercial break, this is what Lloyd, his guests, and all other Cubs' fans heard on the local radio station:

"Good evening, again, baseball fans of every description and welcome to tonight's winner-take-all game between the home team Chicago Cubs and the visiting Reds.

"The events leading up to tonight's game could hardly be more dramatic, but the final act of this drama is the game itself that is scheduled to begin in just ten minutes.

"In spite of injuries to several of the Cub's usual starting cast, we are hoping for a close, competitive contest. It will certainly be a well watched and well listened to game, regardless of the final outcome. The events preceding tonight's broadcast have piqued the interest of not just this country, but the entire world. I was told prior to tonight's game that there are an estimated two billion people either watching or listening to this game, making it the single-largest worldwide audience for any athletic contest, including all prior World Cup Soccer finals. As I look through the press box area and listen to the dialogue among various announcers, I can hear nine different languages.

"Our broadcast, of course, will be in English, as is my custom, and I'll do my best to describe the action, although I'm not sure any language or any broadcaster would be an even match for the tension and excitement in the air that is literally beyond description.

"Those of you who have been to Wrigley Field are familiar with the deep left field fence and the even deeper power alley in left center. In spite of those distances, the Reds' power hitters in the 3, 4, and 5 positions put on quite a show during batting practice. Even the Cubs' players were entertained while standing on their dugout steps and in the bullpen watching ball after ball disappear over the left field wall.

"I suspect that at least part of the Reds' batting practice effort was geared toward catching the eye of the Cubs' surprise starter for tonight's game, Fred Farley. Fred is impressive to the eye himself, standing six feet six inches tall, with broad shoulders and a strong right arm. Those of you following the Cubs' farm system teams know that Fred is primarily a power pitcher with a fastball measuring in the mid-90s. In spite of his impressive arm strength and imposing stature, Fred's dominant physical characteristic is considered by many to be his handlebar mustache, measuring by some accounts, at an even eight inches in length from tip to tip.

"Some of the local sports writers have been critical of the Cubs' manager, Russ Freeman, for starting Fred instead of one of the veteran pitchers in the Cubs' starting rotation. Based on what I know and have heard about Fred Farley, however, I think Russ's selection of the starting pitcher is a calculated gamble that could pay off for the Cubs' second-year manager. Time will tell whether the Reds will take advantage of the rookie pitcher's possible nervousness or whether Fred can succeed in the art of intimidation in the big leagues in the same way that has made him a minor-league legend in the few short weeks he has been pitching at the Triple-A level.

"The natural grass playing surface in the infield and outfield at Wrigley Field has been crosscut to perfection for tonight's game by the Cubs' groundskeeper, Sands McElroy, in anticipation of the national (or should I say 'global') television viewing audience. Hopefully, many of those viewers will be turning down the sound and listening to the Cubs' radio network. Whether you are watching, listening, or both, be advised that playing conditions are perfect. In addition to an immaculate field of play, Mother Nature has also set a perfect stage for tonight's game with cloudless skies and a current temperature of 72 degrees Fahrenheit. Venus and the moon have been dancing in a rare conjunction over the right field stands for almost thirty minutes before game time and are currently ascending in the evening sky as if trying to get a better view of tonight's festivities.

"Sands McElroy's crew just finished the ceremonial lining of the batter's box and the first and third base foul lines. Those finishing touches were followed by the umpires' gathering at home plate for the traditional exchange of starting lineups between the opposing team managers. The ground rules have been given to both managers by the umpire crew chief, Fats Fitzsimmons.

"At this time, I would like to open the crowd microphone for the singing of our national anthem by the Illinois State High School Choir."

At Lloyd's house, all the guests were listening to every word of Red's broadcast. When the national anthem began, no one treated it as an unimportant part of the pregame ritual. In their community, the lines separating love for country and love for the national pastime were blurred. The two were part of the same fabric. Lloyd's wife, Louise, commented that she knew someone whose daughter was a member of the all-state choir, though she couldn't remember the daughter's name at the moment.

". . . and the home . . . of the . . . brave."

The crowd noise was deafening, and the stadium microphone brought the entire stands of Wrigley Field into Lloyd's house.

Red Trickey continued:

"Normally, all of the members of the Cubs' team stand during the national anthem. Tonight, however, I saw two members of the team and two of the coaches sitting during our country's anthem, not out of disrespect for the flag, but because they are in wheel chairs.

"As many of you know, Commissioner O'Malley ruled that the Cubs could expand their roster to 30 from the usual 24 for tonight's game due to the team's injuries from the airplane crash landing two days ago. He also ruled that all members of the Cubs' team and coaching staff could actively participate in the game by sitting in the expanded dugout for this evening's contest, even if they are physically unable to play. That means, therefore, that there are an assortment of crutches, wheel chairs, and casts to complement the usual dugout paraphernalia of bats, gloves, and balls. From this angle, the Cubs' dugout looks more like the waiting room of an orthopedic surgeon's office than a baseball dugout, but there are at least nine healthy bodies ready to take the field, even though four of them have never participated in any regular season major-league game, much less a game of this magnitude.

"Fats Fitzsimmons has assumed his position behind home plate. The home team is taking the field. Due to the roar of the crowd, I can't hear his voice, but I suspect that Fats just said 'Play Ball.'"

Everyone at Lloyd's house sat back with quiet anticipation for the game to begin. Red continued the broadcast saying:

"The home team Cubs have taken the field and Fred Farley has just finished his warm-up tosses under the watchful eye of Tommy Thompson, the Reds' veteran leadoff hitter. Pudge Jones, the Cubs' catcher for tonight's game, who only arrived to the team yesterday from the Triple-A farm club where he threw out 72 of 92 attempted base stealers, guns the ball to Tiny Martin at second, who flips to Scooter Stanford at short, over to first, and back to third for the first of many around the horns in tonight's game.

"The crowd noise is registering at least a 9.9 on a scale of 10, as Fred toes the rubber and looks in for the sign. Fasten your seat belts as we await the first pitch of the last game of the year for one of these two teams. There is not much doubt what the first pitch will be as Fred rocks and fires a fastball that is low and away for ball one.

"Fred has pretty good control for a power pitcher, but the Cubs' coaches are privately concerned that the pressure of tonight's game could present a problem in his getting the ball over the plate consistently.

"Tommy Thompson sets up well back in the batter's box for the next pitch. Here's the windup and the throw. Oh! Watch out! A little chin music sends Mr. Thompson flying backward out of the box and sprawling on the ground.

"The home plate umpire, Fats Fitzsimmons, has walked around to the front of the plate pointing his ample posterior to the pitcher's mound while leaning over to dust off the plate. Fats could be saying something to the rookie catcher, but it is unlikely that Fred is throwing a message pitch this early in the game, especially one sending the count to 2 and 0.

"Meanwhile, Ace Simmons, the Reds' manager, has walked to the top of his team's dugout steps and seems to be gesturing towards the pitcher's mound. I doubt if he's asking Fred if he'd like to go out to eat after the game.

"Tommy Thompson has dusted himself off and steps back into the box to wait for the next offering. Fred takes a deep breath and goes into a full windup and throws the next pitch . . . way high and at least a foot outside.

"The batter was bailing out on that pitch almost before the ball was released. I can't say as I blame him, given the fact that the last pitch was clocked at 96 miles per hour on the gun. That kind of speed and no control is a real attention getter if your only defense is a wooden stick and quick feet.

"If Fred can gain his composure and control, this display of wildness might help him later in the game by making the batters wary for their safety, but right now it spells trouble. He doesn't want to issue Tommy Thompson an automatic pass to open the game because he's leading the American League in stolen bases with an incredible 127 steals in 142 attempts.

"Fred takes a deep sigh and dips down for the resin bag which he throws fiercely to the turf behind the pitcher's mound, sending a white cloud mushrooming three feet up from the ground.

"The pitcher toes the rubber and begins his windup. The batter squares around as if to bunt and watches ball four low and in.

"Oh my! This could spell trouble early for the young pitcher. Pudge Jones calls time and hustles out to the mound. Mark Yudof, the most senior infielder with over 10 years of experience, walks over from first and has a word with the rookie pitcher. There is no movement in the Cubs' dugout, and I'm sure Russ does not want to waste his free trip to the mound this early in the inning.

"Fats Fitzsimmons has walked toward the mound to break up the gathering, and we are just about ready to resume play. The second batter in the Cubs' lineup is Merv Wallace, who steps in batting .326 for the year.

"Tommy Thompson takes a hefty leadoff first as Fred backs off the rubber looking at the runner. Turk McGhee, the Cubs' Triple-A pitching coach who is on the coaching staff for tonight's game, told me yesterday that Fred does not have much of a move to first although he is rather quick for a big man. He has picked off only one runner this year during his stint with the Cubs' Triple-A organization.

"Merv Wallace stands back in the box awaiting the pitch. Tommy Thompson extends his lead and is off with a pitch that is low and away. Pudge catches the ball cleanly and throws toward second. The throw is high and gets by Scooter Stanford, who was covering the bag. Thompson pops up immediately from his slide and is speeding toward third. Fortunately, Wheels Wilson, playing in center, was backing up the throw, and Thompson is not able to advance any further than third.

"Well, this is not exactly what Cubs' fans had in mind for the opening of this game, and the crowd has quieted considerably. The count stands 1 and 0 with a runner on third as the next pitch comes in. It is also outside the strike zone. Fred Farley has thrown six straight balls to the first two batters of the game.

"Things are serious early at Wrigley Field. Tommy Thompson is taking a long lead at third and begins a bluff down the third base line trying to coax the rookie into a balk. Fred steps off the rubber, and the runner retreats. That is a good sign in that the young pitcher is not so rattled as to fall for one of the oldest tricks in the books.

"Fred steps back on the rubber, eyes the batter, and fires. The pitch is again outside the strike zone, although that time, it was closer than any previous pitch. That is seven straight balls to open the game.

"There is still no sign of action in the Cubs' bullpen, and Russ Freeman has not moved from his usual seat in the dugout. I have not watched Fred pitch this year, but it seems to me that he is working a bit fast.

"The runner at third again bluffs down the line as Fred throws the next pitch. Ball four. That appeared to be a curve ball but it had no better luck finding the strike zone than its seven fastball predecessors. Runners are now at the corners with nobody out and no score in the top of the first with the Reds batting.

"Russ Freeman, the Cubs' manager, still has not stirred from his usual position in the dugout, but I thought I saw him nod to Turk McGhee, the rookie right-hander's minor-league pitching coach, who also has moved up to the big leagues for this game due to the plane crash injury to his major-league counterpart, Mike Mason. Mike Mason, as those of you carefully following the plane crash injury list know, is one of four Cubs' players or coaches still in the hospital after the accident.

"Turk has moved to the top step of the Cubs' dugout and now makes a move out of the dugout and toward the pitcher's mound, where he will be joined by the catcher, Pudge Jones, and all the infielders.

"Turk McGhee is as short as Fred Farley is tall and watching the two men talk eye to eye is a study in contrast with Turk's being at least a foot shorter than his young protégé. It would be interesting to know exactly what is being said between the two."

On the field, away from all ears except the six Cubs' players gathered at the pitcher's mound, Turk was doing all the talking. He was not loud or demonstrative as he said, "I want you to consciously take at least ten more seconds between pitches than you have been. The only thing wrong is that you are in too much of a hurry."

"Pudge," he said to the catcher, "in order to do your part to slow things down, wait a few seconds before giving him the sign for the next pitch. Also, remember who is coming up. Don Nelson is primarily a fastball hitter. Fred, I want you to start him out with a curve. Keep throwing your hook until you get a strike and then follow the strike with heat and then go back to the curve when you have two strikes on him.

"Do you have any questions?"

There was a pause.

"No," said Fred.

"I know you can do it," said Turk. "Oh, and one more thing. Start spitting more often between pitches." Everyone grinned at that last comment. Turk hoped it would loosen his pitcher up some. He gave Fred a firm pat on the behind and turned to trot back to the dugout just as Fats Fitzsimmons was walking slowly toward the mound to break up the meeting.

At Lloyd's house, the air of excitement and hope for the game was beginning to turn to concern and despair when the announcer continued his comments, saying:

"Fats Fitzsimmons has wheeled and turned back towards home plate after breaking up the infield convention on the mound. The Reds' next batter is Don Nelson, who is batting .339 for the year with 28 home runs and 135 RBIs.

"Fred Farley is leaning in for the sign, looks toward third and then looks toward first. Neither runner shows any sign of advancing. Fred is working from the stretch position which might make it even more difficult for him to find a rhythm early. I suspect that the batter does not have the take sign, but we'll soon find out if the ball is thrown over the plate. Fred winds and throws. It's a swing and a miss for strike one. The pitch was a slow curve, and Don Nelson was obviously thinking fastball. Just as obviously, he was thinking about a three-run dinger, judging by the ferocity of his swing. I thought I saw the flags that are blowing in the outfield stands shift slightly with the whoosh of air from Nelson's bat as he turned on the ball.

"The crowd has responded noisily to the first strike of the game. Fred stands ready to throw the next pitch, but does not seem to be in as much of a hurry this time as he was with the first two batters. I would not be surprised if Turk told his charge to slow down between pitches.

"The pitcher leans in, nods approval of the sign, rocks, and fires.

"It's a called strike two!

"That time, Don Nelson looked to be sitting on a curve ball, but what he got was anything but a curve. That ball measured 97 miles per hour on the radar gun and appeared to be over the outside part of the plate, knee high. Listen to these fans roar their approval."

Lloyd Stevens loved the crowd sounds on the radio. He had listened to enough baseball on the radio to be able to tell what had just happened on the field even before Red described it, but he still enjoyed listening to Red Trickey's radio description of the action. He also appreciated the fact that Red would just stop talking on occasion and let his audience listen to the fans who were watching in person. Those snitches of crowd noise during the course of a game were not as readily available with a duo announcer team as with a single broadcaster because usually one of the two was always talking.

Lloyd looked around the room. Supper plates were still half full, but no one was chewing food. Everyone was waiting in anticipation for the next pitch when Red continued his broadcast, saying:

"The fans are on their feet at Wrigley Field. This is just the third batter of the first inning, but the crowd senses this could be a pivotal part of the game. Fred Farley has walked a few steps toward his dugout and seems to be looking at his teammates as he spits once, twice, and, for good measure, three times, before walking back to the rubber. Let's hope that's three times for three strikes. He's glaring in for the sign from the catcher who is not yet even looking at the pitcher's mound.

"Now the two men comprising the Cubs' battery are facing each other as Don Nelson steps back into the batter's box and takes the obligatory warm-up swings. The pitcher glares toward first and looks the runner back as he steps off the rubber.

"The cycle repeats itself as the crowd noise builds again. Here comes the pitch. Strike three called! Another big, sweeping, curve ball that immobilized the batter. Don Nelson shakes his head in disgust as he beats his bat into the grass on his way back to the dugout. He has not failed many times to drive in a run in situations like that this year, but this time, he did fail and the home crowd roars its approval."

Food was flying at Lloyd Stevens' house as the guests celebrated with high fives and laughter.

In the Cubs' dugout, Turk beamed. Russ's face bore a slight grin, but he did not change his position in the dugout. He knew the cleanup batter for the Reds, Oak Hogan, represented an even bigger threat than Don Nelson had.

Red Trickey continued, "Pudge, the Cubs' catcher, guns the ball back to his fellow minor leaguer with whom he is sharing this dream. Speaking of dreams, please don't wake me up until tonight is over. This game—the whole season—the events of the last two days—are prime ingredients for dreams. Oh, what a night!

"The cleanup batter for the Reds steps into the batter's box. He's looking menacingly toward the mound. Fred Farley is looking back just as fiercely as he spits again in the general direction of home plate. If they were not separated by 60 feet 6 inches, you'd think they were two heavyweight fighters getting prefight instructions from the referee.

"Pudge Jones has looked toward the dugout for pitch selection instructions, and he now squats to give the sign. Fred nods his head in approval, and here comes the pitch. There's a long fly ball, deep toward center! Wheels Wilson, the new center fielder for the Cubs, has turned his back completely on home plate and is racing toward the fence. That ball may be out of here. Holy horse! He reaches up and makes the grab over his right shoulder!

"The runner at third was tagging all the way, and he'll score easily, but the runner on first is already past second. He will have to retrace his tracks by stepping on second on his way back to first. The throw from center is a perfect strike to the shortstop who had gone out toward center to accept the relay throw. Scooter

Stanford turns and fires toward first. He's out at first base! Holy horse! What a play! Listen to the crowd."

For the next thirty seconds, all Lloyd Stevens could hear was yelling and screaming. It was difficult to separate the noise made by his guests from the roar of the radios. After the crowd noise paused, Red Trickey recapped the play describing the center fielder's legs as he was running for the ball by comparing them to the "pistons on an eight-cylinder car going 20 miles over the speed limit on a straight, flat highway." The announcer continued, saying:

"The Reds have drawn first blood by scoring a run, but the crowd is still in a frenzy with that spectacular catch and throw from the center fielder. That's two walks, one strikeout and one well hit ball, but only one run for the Reds in the top of the first as we pause for these messages from our sponsors."

After between inning advertisements, Red Trickey continued his telecast.

"Welcome back, baseball fans, to Wrigley Field, where we were treated to high drama in the top of the first inning with the Reds scoring only one run due to a spectacular catch and throw by the Cubs' first-day rookie center fielder, Wheels Wilson.

"The Reds' pitcher for tonight's game is Stuben Mitchell. Over the last three seasons, Mitchell has had a spectacular 12 and 0 against the Cubs. That does not bode well for this evening's contest. On the other hand, maybe a Cubs' win is long overdue against the big right-hander.

"Mitchell has finished taking his warm-up tosses and the Reds' veteran catcher, Roy Wood, guns the ball down to second base where the second baseman takes the throw, flips to short, who throws to first and then to third to complete the Reds' opening around the horn.

"As Wheels Wilson, the Cubs' center fielder, steps into the batter's box, I am reminded of one of the game's best-known and colorful baseball announcers of years ago, Dizzy Dean, who worked the Saturday Game of the Week for so many years with his broadcast companion, Pee Wee Reese. Dizzy was fond of saying, 'Oh, Pee Wee, as happens so many times in this game of baseball, the player who ends the inning with a spectacular fielding play leads off to bat the next inning.'

"Wilson's play was, indeed, spectacular, and he is leading off in the bottom of this opening stanza with the Cubs down one to zero. Wheels Wilson has joined the team for this his first game in the major leagues from the Cubs Double-A farm club in Tennessee, where he batted a very respectable .325 as a switch hitter. More importantly, he has speed to burn in that he has stolen a Double-A record 98 bases in 105 attempts. Thank goodness for that speed last inning with his remarkable, over the shoulder grab of Oak Hogan's long drive to dead center field.

"Stuben Mitchell is just as imposing physically as his counterpart, Fred Farley. Stuben has no mustache but considerably more credentials. In this his eighth year in the league, he is a consensus Hall of Famer, sporting an amazing three Cy Young awards over his relatively short major-league career.

"Wheels Wilson has assumed his crouched batting stance against the big right-hander. He is batting from the left side. His fingers are rippling over the bat handle in a loose grip as he awaits Mitchell's first offering that is on its way.

"The first pitch in the bottom of the first is a hard strike over the outside corner of the plate. The radar gun clocked that pitch at 94 miles per hour. Wilson probably didn't see many pitches like that in Double-A ball, especially ones combining mid-90s velocity with pinpoint control painting the black outside part of the plate.

"Wheels Wilson stands back in for the second offering as Mitchell rocks and fires in his classic high-leg kick delivery reminiscent of Juan Marichal.

"Wheels drops his bat and places a bunt perfectly down the third base line! With his high-leg kick, Mitchell does not finish his delivery in good fielding position and that ball squirted just past his outstretched glove, where it was fielded on a slow roll by the third baseman, who did not even bother to throw to first.

"The speedy Wilson has his first big-league hit, and the Cubs are in business with a runner on first base and no one out in the bottom of the first inning trailing by a run.

"Well, get ready for the cat-and-mouse game between Mitchell and Wilson. This is the situation Russ Freeman was hoping for when he invited the Double-A rookie base-stealing sensation to play tonight in place of Steve Pettis, the Cubs' injured center fielder.

"Like his counterpart, Fred Farley, Mitchell does not have a particularly good move to first. I've already mentioned his high-leg kick which slows his delivery to the plate, although it's slightly less exaggerated when he's working from the stretch position. The catcher, Roy Wood, leads the league in caught stealings.

"The fans in sold-out Wrigley Field increase the noise level as they anticipate this classic matchup early in the game involving Wheels Wilson and the Reds' pitcher and catcher.

"Mitchell stares in for the sign as Pat Smith, the veteran left fielder, steps in the box. Mitchell checks the runner on first, steps back off the rubber, and throws a soft toss to first, where the runner scampers back ahead of the throw.

"That was not Mitchell's best move. Pat Smith steps back in, and Mitchell addresses home plate while Wilson increases his lead off first. Watch out! This time, Mitchell fired the ball to first and almost caught Wheels' leaning the wrong way. He had to dive back into the bag headfirst just ahead of the slap tag by the first baseman. That was close.

"Wheels Wilson calls time and stands up to dust the infield dirt off his new uniform. He's probably taking a deep sigh of relief that he was not called out on that close play. We'll see how much that close call shortens his lead when we resume play.

"Mitchell toes the rubber again, glares to first, and then begins his delivery motion. This time, the pitch comes toward home as Wilson takes off for second. It's a foul ball into the stands behind the plate; strike one.

"Wilson did not appear to have a good jump on the ball as Russ Freeman plays hit-and-run early in the game. I believe the runner's lead was shortened due to the prior close play at first.

"Big Stuben Mitchell stands behind the pitcher's mound rubbing down the new baseball thrown to him by Fats Fitzsimmons. Wheels Wilson stands on first, waiting for one of the many games within the game to begin anew.

"Both the batter and the base runner are looking at the third base coach, Windmill Betherd, who is flashing signs in his characteristic exaggerated style loved by fans of all ages. He has more body language than Jerry Lewis as he goes through the rhythmic motions of touching virtually every body part with both hands between pitches.

"Wheels Wilson and Pat Smith seem satisfied they have understood the secret meaning contained in the third base coach's dancelike display as they ready themselves for the next pitch.

"Mitchell, oblivious to everything but the task at hand, stares in for the sign, glances toward first, and throws toward home. The ball is again hit foul, this time slowly down the first base line, where it comes to rest just even with the first base bag. Wilson, who was again off and running with the pitch, walks slowly back to first as the ball is retrieved by the Cubs' first base coach, Rick Rogers. Rogers examines the ball closely, wags his hand holding the ball four or five times back and forth to signify that it was scuffed on the play and tosses it out of play softly into the stands behind the first base dugout. Throwing the ball out of play and into the stands like that costs each player or coach who does it $2 per ball. If statistics were kept, the Cubs probably would lead the league in souvenirs thrown into the stands.

"Mitchell begins the ritual of rubbing down a new ball as the count stands at 0 and 2, with a runner on first, nobody out, and the Cubs trailing 1 to 0.

"Pat Smith stands in and is ready for the next pitch. Mitchell again checks the runner at first and throws to the plate as the runner breaks for second base. The ball is outside and high. The batter swings to protect the runner and misses for strike three. Here's the throw. *He's safe!* Wheels Wilson calls time and picks himself up and dusts himself off . . . as the song goes.

"Pat Smith, a strikeout victim, walks dejectedly back to the Cubs' dugout. He probably swung at a bad ball, but the motion of his bat kept the Reds' all-star catcher honest and slowed his catch and throw to second enough to give the speeding Wilson time to perform a beautiful hook slide toward the right field side of the bag just out of reach of the tag at second.

"The Cubs have a little something going as the team's regular third baseman, Guns Gleaton, steps to the plate batting .307 for the year with 112 RBIs. You know he's thinking about number 113 as he takes his warm-up swings.

"In case you're wondering, 23 of Wilson's 98 stolen bases have been of third base. Most accomplished base stealers contend that it's easier to steal third than second because it's easier to get a longer lead; but I think it's doubtful he'll be going in this situation since he's already in scoring position with only one out.

"Mitchell is still throwing from the stretch position as he rocks and fires toward the plate. The ball is hit on the ground toward the hole between short and third. Even though the ball was hit in front of him, Wilson is streaking toward third. The ball is fielded on a dive by the shortstop, who has no play at first. He guns the ball from a kneeling position to third. Wilson slides headfirst on the home plate side of the base. He's safe! The throw was slightly on the outfield side of the bag, but I'm not sure a perfect throw would have been good enough.

"Wheels Wilson violated one of the cardinal base running rules by leaving second with the ball hit on the ground toward the third base side, but he got away with a mistake borne of enthusiasm and inexperience because he is so fast.

"Listen to the crowd. They are vibrating out of their seats early tonight at Wrigley Field.

"Runners are at the corners as Tonic Tisdale, the club's cleanup hitter, steps to the plate. They are standing in the stadium as Mitchell toes the rubber and begins his delivery. Tonic takes a huge swing and misses badly for a 0 and 1 count.

"Tonic was thinking fastball, and he got a slow curve instead. He stands with his front foot out of the box as he adjusts his batting gloves. He looks down to the third base coach, but Windmill Betherd is eerily still. Tonic is on his own with neither a hit-and-run nor a squeeze play planned. The situation is power pitcher versus power hitter as Mitchell prepares to throw the second pitch to the fourth batter of Chicago's half of the first inning. The crowd has quieted some with the swinging strike on the last pitch. Here comes the second pitch to the cleanup hitter. There's a long fly ball deep to right! The Reds right fielder is not even retreating on the ball. He just looks up as the ball sails into the third tier of the right field bleachers! It's Tater Time at the Cubs' home park.

"Tonic Tisdale has just hit his 438th major-league home run, and I suspect he'd say that's the biggest one of his career.

"Wheels Wilson jogs home with the first run, where he waits for his new teammates to round the bases. Guns Gleaton steps on home for the second run and is followed by a smiling Tonic Tisdale, who finishes his home run trot for the Cubs' third run of the inning.

"The crowd begins their rhythmic chant of 'Give it back,' exhorting their fellow fans in the right field stands to throw the ball back onto the playing surface. And here it comes! The ball is tossed back toward the right fielder, completing one of the many traditions established by the Cubs' fans. The ball's return flight to the playing field was in slow motion compared to its exit. The Reds' right fielder retrieves the ball, and in a gesture of good sportsmanship, throws it into the Cubs' bullpen area, where I'm sure it will eventually make its way to Tonic Tisdale's trophy case.

"The Cubs take the lead for the first time in tonight's game, and, if memory serves, for the first time this year against Stuben Mitchell, who, as I said earlier, has not lost to the Cubs in 3 years. This game, of course, is a long way from over, but the Cub fans are savoring the moment and they are refusing to quiet down until Tonic comes out for a curtain call. There he is, head emerging at the top of the home team dugout for a brief doffing of his cap.

"So, with one down and the Cubs on top 3 to 1 in the bottom of the first inning, the Cubs' first baseman, veteran Mark Yudof, steps to the plate as the crowd catches their collective breath. As you probably know, Mark Yudof is normally the Cubs' backup first baseman, but he has been pressed into service because of the plane crash injury suffered by Wilson Smith. Wilson is expected to enjoy a full recovery from his broken ribs and cracked tibia in his left leg, but, of course, he is out for tonight's game and the remainder of postseason play. If the Cubs can hold on to this early lead, they will be part of postseason play for the first time in their history.

"Mitchell is pitching now from a full windup. Here's the pitch. It's a fastball over the middle of the plate for strike one. The Reds' catcher, Roy Wood, throws the ball back to Mitchell.

"Mitchell, who is a fast worker to begin with, appears impatient to deliver the next pitch. He is still fuming from Tonic Tisdale's three-run blast. He rocks and fires. Yudof takes a ferocious swing but comes up empty for strike two.

"Yudof was thinking fastball all the way. He got it, but was unable to make contact with Mitchell's pitch, which, I'm told, registered 96 miles per hour on the gun. His arm is smoking as much as his temper.

"Both players are ready for the 0-2 pitch. Mitchell nods his approval of the sign from Roy Wood. Here's the pitch. Yudof swings again but is way out in front of an off-speed curve ball. Swinging strike three. Now there are two outs, with the Cubs' catcher for tonight's game, Pudge Jones, coming to the plate.

"Pudge was called up from the team's Triple-A farm club, where he and Fred Farley were roommates on road trips. The Cubs' usual catcher, Legs Cooper, is one of the many plane crash victims unable to play in tonight's game due to injury. Russ Freeman told me that he considered giving the start tonight to the Cubs' backup catcher, Stubbs Mahew, but decided that Fred Farley might be more comfortable throwing to his usual battery mate, Pudge Jones.

"Pudge steps in sporting a healthy .348 Triple-A batting average for the year. He bats from the right side. This is his third year in the Cubs' organization, having been drafted in the first round out of the graduating class of one of Coach Clif Gustafson's University of Texas baseball squads. He has made his way steadily through the farm teams from the rookie league in his first year all the way up to Triple-A this year. Now, of course, he has unexpectedly completed his journey to the big leagues due to the bizarre happenings of the last three days.

"The Cubs' baseball scouts tell me he is the heir apparent to Legs if Legs retires as expected at the end of his contract in 2 years.

"Stuben Mitchell is still stomping around behind the pitcher's mound but now turns toward home plate and toes the rubber. Here comes his first offering. It's another slow curve that completely froze the Cubs' young catcher. The ball was right over the inside corner of the plate for strike one.

"Mitchell is again working quickly. He looks in for the sign, rocks, and fires. Strike two on a swing and a miss. That time, it looked as if Mitchell threw a slider.

"Stuben Mitchell has five different pitches, which is one of the things that makes him so effective. He throws a curve, a changeup, a fastball, the slider that he just showed to Pudge Jones, and he's also been experimenting with a new pitch he calls the split-finger fastball that we'll probably see before this game is over. In fact, he frequently throws the splitter with a two-strike count when there are two or fewer balls and no one on base. It would not surprise me if we see the split finger on this next offering.

"Here comes the pitch. It's the splitter down and out of the strike zone, but Pudge was fooled again and he weakly swung at strike three. The ball was not caught cleanly by the catcher, and he gathers it in and tosses it to first base to officially record the out.

"So, the side is retired, but not before the Cubs score 3 runs in the bottom of the first on three hits, the big one being Tonic Tisdale's three-run home run. There were no errors. We go to the top of the second with the Cubs leading 3 to 1. We'll return to Cubs' baseball after these commercial messages."

Chapter 11

THE EVENING BEFORE THE GAME, June, Madge, Wallis, and Sylvia had sponsored a buffet in the private dining room of a local Mexican food restaurant for all the mothers, wives, and kids of the Cubs' players and coaches. They had wasted no time welcoming the new additions to their baseball family. June had convinced Deep Pockets to make his contribution to the cohesiveness of the group by donating 100 extra game tickets to add to the usual allotment of 200 seats for the players' family and friends. Most of the seats were located behind the home team dugout on the third base side of the diamond. By game time, the immediate family members were becoming one in spirit just as their player counterparts were becoming a team.

The stress and emotion of the first inning further strengthened the unity of the 300 family members and close friends gathered in the Cubs' family section. They were filled with enthusiasm and hope after the home team's three runs in the bottom of the first.

Not long after Fred Farley took the mound for the top of the second, their original fears of losing returned as the Reds' number five hitter smashed the first pitch he saw into the left field stands for a solo home run.

Their spirits, and the noise level in the stadium, rose again, though, as Fred Farley struck out the next three batters.

In the bottom of the second, Stuben Mitchell matched Fred Farley's strikeouts of the top half of the inning with three consecutive strikeouts of his own. The score stood 3 to 2 in favor of the Cubs after two innings of play.

The players' and coaches' wives, family members, and friends watched as neither team could mount a serious offensive threat in the third inning. After three innings, the score remained 3 to 2, Cubs.

Fred Farley walked the first batter in the top of the fourth inning, but the runner was promptly erased when the next batter hit a sharp ground ball up the middle to the shortstop, who stepped on second and fired the ball to first for the game's initial double play.

Fred followed his infielders' superb play with another strikeout, his sixth of the game, to end the Reds' half of the fourth inning. June was smiling and laughing from her seat in the middle of the family section. Her husband's gamble with Fred Farley was paying off, and she was as relieved as she was happy. There was, of course, a long way to go in the game, but things were going well for the home team.

In the Cubs' half of the fourth, Tonic was the leadoff batter. The crowd stood as one for his at bat, but he struck out, swinging on a hard slider with the count full.

In the first inning when Tonic hit a three-run homer, everyone in the family section had turned to congratulate Sylvia Tisdale. After the strikeout in the fourth, Madge said, "That's OK." Wallis patted Sylvia on the back, and June clinched Sylvia's hand reassuringly. June often told her husband that the pressure of watching a loved one in a key situation during a game was an even greater burden than being the athlete in the spotlight. Baseball was filled with ups and downs . . . through a game, a season, and a career. It helped to share the ups and downs with friends and relatives. After receiving her friends' reassurances, Sylvia turned her energy toward supporting Nancy Yudof, the wife of the reserve first baseman, Mark Yudof, who was the next batter.

As each wife, girlfriend, mom, daughter, or son took his turn watching his player field a ball, make a throw, or take a turn at bat, June realized that she felt pressure for each player's success or failure because her husband would be given credit or blame for the total performance.

Mark Yudof proceeded to foul off three pitches on a 3 and 2 count before walking on a high fastball. He trotted toward first base as Pudge Jones, the young Triple-A catcher, took his warm-up swings for his second at bat.

Pudge's wife and his mother were sitting in front of June. June put her hands on their shoulders as Pudge stepped into the batter's box. Mark Yudof was not a threat to steal, so he was not taking a long lead at first. The crowd noise increased again. Everyone sensed that Stuben Mitchell was not on top of his game. The home crowd's anticipation was soon rewarded as Pudge sliced the first offering down the right field line and into the irregularly angled right field corner where the ball virtually stopped dead. The scouting report on Pudge was that he pulled the ball, and the right fielder had been playing toward center. By the time the right fielder reached the ball, Mark Yudof had rounded third and Pudge Jones was almost all the way to third base. As the ball came into the infield, Yudof scored and Pudge stood on third with a stand-up triple. The crowd roared its approval. The score was now 4 to 2 in favor of the home team. There was one out in the bottom of the fourth with Pudge Jones on third and Scooter Stanford coming to the plate.

June, Madge, Wallis, Sylvia, and all the family members and friends in the family section were exchanging hugs and high fives. Fans in adjacent sections began to imitate the wives' behavior and strangers united in a common bond of excitement at the prospect of winning a division title after years of frustration.

The next batter, who was a first-game rookie shortstop, added to the fans' frenzy as he and Pudge perfectly executed a safety squeeze play, with Pudge scoring on a bunted ball down the first base side. June beamed with happiness. The textbook success of the first few innings were a tribute to a well coached and well prepared team. She looked around her section, at the stadium, and toward Venus and the moon. She enjoyed the moment of having just watched the successful execution of one of baseball's most aggressive offensive strategies, a squeeze play, with the quiet pride of knowing that her husband had toppled over the first domino, resulting in the fans' current exhilaration.

Tiny Martin, the number 8 hitter, walked, but Fred Farley grounded out on a fielder's choice to end the inning. The first four innings were in the books with a promising 5 to 2, Cubs' lead. Stuben Mitchell was still in the game, but tonight, he was not untouchable.

Chapter 12

IN THE CUBS' DUGOUT, RUSS had barely changed his expression or position during the first four innings. He had walked over to Turk McGhee between the third and fourth inning to whisper thanks for Turk's accurate prediction of Fred's readiness for such a pressure-packed game.

During their brief exchange, Turk told Russ that Fred had barely slept the night before. Plus, Turk said that Fred's velocity was even faster than usual. Turk predicted that Fred might not be able to go more than six innings and suggested they keep a close eye on him.

The top of the fifth inning began in a favorable way for Fred with two straight strikes to the number 9 hitter in the order, one swinging and one called. On the next three pitches, however, Fred missed the plate high and away to push the count full. Russ squirmed uneasily in his seat and glanced at Turk, who was closely following his young pitcher's motions.

The next two pitches were fouled off. The final pitch to the first batter in the top of the 5th was ball 4. The batter trotted toward first.

Russ knew that the runner was a threat to steal and considered calling for a pitchout on the first pitch to the next batter, but he decided against it because he thought Fred might be experiencing control problems. Russ did not want to increase the pressure of throwing strikes by requiring Fred to waste a pitch.

Even though the score was 5 to 2, Russ knew that things could change quickly as the Reds moved to the top of their order with a man on first.

The runner was taking a long lead off first when Fred abruptly stepped off the rubber and fired the ball to first base. The runner, who, no doubt, had read a scouting report on Fred saying that he had a mediocre move, was clearly surprised. The throw was in perfect position, and Mark Yudof made a swipe tag. The first base umpire pointed the index finger of his right hand toward the first base bag and followed the point with an emphatic "out" call and a punching bag motion with his right fist. Russ found himself caught up in the excitement of the successful pick-off play. He was not alone. The home team crowd yelled approval as the ball was gunned around the infield and back to Fred, who glared at the batter before resuming his pitching position.

Russ watched and listened as Fred struck out the next batter on five pitches. The pitch count was now up to 90 and Russ was still concerned about Fred's tiring, but he relaxed a bit because it looked like Fred might get through the fifth without giving up another run. As a precaution, however, he phoned down to the Cubs' bullpen and told the bullpen catcher to warm up Hooks and a left-handed relief pitcher.

No sooner had he hung up the phone than the Reds' number 2 batter singled sharply to left. As the crowd stirred restlessly, Fred stomped around behind the pitching mound. When he resumed his pitching position, Russ climbed to the top of the dugout and began a slow walk to the pitcher's mound. In a time-honored tradition, Russ was planning to stall for time to give his bullpen pitchers a chance to warm up.

Russ noticed Fats Fitzsimmons out of the corner of his eye and knew that Fats would not let him erect a tent on the pitcher's mound, but he also knew that Fats would give him at least thirty seconds before walking to the mound to break things up. As Russ reached Fred, he was joined by Pudge and the entire Cubs' infield.

In his usual direct way, Russ said, "I want to know how your arm feels. I know you want to pitch, or I wouldn't have started you, but I need to know whether you're tired so I can include your thoughts before making a decision about bringing in a relief pitcher."

"I'm not tired," said Fred. "My velocity is still good, but my control is a little off."

"Here's what I want you to do," Russ said as he saw Fats beginning his amble to the mound. "Work very slowly to the next batter. Throw over to first at least three times before you throw a pitch to the plate. Remember, Don Nelson is a low fastball hitter. Work him outside starting with a slider and then come back inside with heat. Got it?"

"Yes, sir," said Fred as Fats reached the mound.

"Just leaving," Russ said to Fats as he turned to walk back to the dugout.

As instructed, Fred tossed the ball to first on three consecutive pick-off throws even though it was obvious that the runner wasn't going anywhere. Meanwhile, Hooks worked feverishly in the bullpen.

The first pitch to the plate to the next batter, Don Nelson, was a slider low and away that was taken for a ball. Russ was glad to see that Fred was working deliberately.

The next pitch was a fastball down and in. Don Nelson turned quickly on the pitch and hit it over the shortstop's head and into left center. The runner on first base had gotten a good jump on the ball so he motored into third easily. There were runners on the corners with two outs and the Reds' cleanup hitter, Oak Hogan, was coming to the plate.

Russ glanced at the bullpen and saw both relief pitchers looking toward the dugout. They were ready. Russ looked at Turk, whose expression confirmed Russ's decision. He stepped to the top of the dugout and walked toward the mound. Halfway there, he motioned to the bullpen and touched his right arm. He was bringing Hooks in to face Oak Hogan.

Fred handed the ball to Russ when he reached the pitcher's mound. Fred waited for Hooks to arrive before going to the dugout. The wait was not long because it was Hooks' custom to run in from the bullpen when called into service. After Russ handed the ball to Hooks, Fred departed the mound to a standing ovation.

Because he did not complete at least five full innings as the starting pitcher, he could not qualify for the win under the official record keeping rules of major-league baseball, but it had been a good outing. The Cubs were ahead 5 to 2 as he left the game, although the two men on base were his responsibility. Fred took a seat in the dugout after receiving his new teammates' congratulations. Russ also returned to the dugout to watch Hooks complete his warm-up throws.

Russ knew from his statistic sheets that Oak Hogan had a lifetime batting average against Hooks of .305. He also knew, however, that his lifetime average against the other bullpen pitchers was a combined .333. He had made the correct statistical choice, but he was still not comfortable with the matchup.

He held his breath as Hooks, working from the stretch position, began his characteristic quick delivery throwing motion. The batter's fingers rose and fell in sequence at the bottom of his bat handle as he waited for the pitch.

Russ watched in horror as the Reds' cleanup batter hit a towering fly ball into deep left center field, where the ball bounced off the top of the fence and back into the playing field. The ball was fielded cleanly by Wheels Wilson, the Cubs' center fielder, but with two outs, both runners were off with the crack of the bat, and both scored easily as Oak Hogan trotted into second with a stand-up double.

The crowd fell silent. The score was now 5 to 4 in favor of the Cubs, but the Reds' number 5 batter was coming to the plate with a runner in scoring position.

Hooks requested a new baseball and Fats obliged. Hooks was standing behind the mound looking at his feet as he rubbed down the new ball. Russ glanced toward the bullpen and saw two pitchers warming up and then looked back at his friend on the mound. He glanced at his statistical sheets and saw the next batter had a lifetime batting average against Hooks of only .175. Russ decided to leave Hooks in the game.

The first pitch to the next hitter gave every hometown fan and Russ a scare as the batter smashed it hard but foul down the first base line. It seemed to Russ that Hooks was working more deliberately than usual. Russ worried that Hooks was out of rhythm because of slowing down too much, but he elected not to make a trip to the mound.

Hooks took a deep breath, and Russ watched as he floated a changeup curve over the outside of the plate for a called strike two. The next pitch was an eye-level fastball that the batter swung at and missed by half a foot for strike three and the third out. The crowd roared its approval. Russ heaved a sigh of relief. After 4½ innings of play, his team was still ahead 5 to 4.

Chapter 13

TWO HUNDRED MILES AWAY AT Lloyd Stevens' family farmhouse, Lloyd, Louise, and their guests also relaxed slightly as the top of the fifth inning came to a close with the Cubs clinging to a one-run lead.

Lloyd Stevens' old RCA radio was working just fine, and his wife's hi-fi radio was also turned up so that everyone in the house could easily listen to the action regardless of which room they were in. Several of his neighbors were also watching the game on his new television set without the sound turned on. Two guests had brought transistor radios. One could be heard on the front porch and the other on the back porch.

Most of the men were sitting in the big living room and following the game with their eyes and ears. Most of the women were outside on the front porch, enjoying the evening breeze and quietly talking while watching some of the younger children play tag in the front yard. Several of the older children were on the back porch or in the bed of Lloyd's pickup listening to the game. The mercury vapor lamp next to the barn had been turned off. The nighttime stars were visible from Lloyd's pickup bed.

Members of all four generations present would occasionally walk into the kitchen to rinse a dish, sample a cookie, or help themselves to a piece of apple pie or chocolate cake.

Before the end of the top of the fifth inning, all the guests but the children playing tag in the front yard were quiet and hanging on each pitch as described by Red Trickey. With the strikeout of the last batter, conversations and smiles broke out inside and outside the house.

Lloyd looked around the living room and saw his 26-year-old son sitting on the floor holding Lloyd's 2-year-old grandson. He stared at the old RCA radio and thought about his father and his grandfather. He reflected on the fact that five generations in his family had listened to baseball games on the same radio.

His gaze returned to his son and grandson. The best way to remember your father, someone had told him when his dad died, is to love your son. Lloyd watched as his son rolled a plastic baseball across the floor and into the outstretched hands of his grandson.

The mood of the gathering exactly followed the fortunes of the Cubs. The Cubs' early 3 to 1 lead had started the evening on a firm foundation of hope. Behind that hope, however, was an undercurrent of fear that this year's season would end with the same disappointment of prior years. In some years, the realization of not being able to finish in first place occurred early in the year. There were other times when the Cubs had been in the race with two weeks to go in the regular season before being mathematically eliminated.

At least when the Cubs were out of the race early, there was ample time to rationalize another losing season. This year, however, there would be no time to prepare sufficiently for finishing second. Everything depended on tonight's game and the next 4½ innings.

Lloyd's fear of the inevitable loss quickly changed back to hope as he listened to Red Trickey's description of the action in the bottom of the fifth. The inning opening strikeout by the Cubs' first batter of the inning was followed by two sharp singles from the veteran left fielder, Pat Smith, and the third baseman, Guns Gleaton.

With runners on first and third and one out, Stuben Mitchell was taken out of the game. There was anticipation by the Cubs' fans as Tonic Tisdale prepared to bat against one of the Reds' best relief pitchers.

To the home crowd's delight, Tonic hit the first pitch over the shortstop's head for a single and another RBI. The runner on first had to stop at second because the ball had been hit hard and was fielded cleanly by the left fielder, who quickly threw it back into the infield.

With runners on first and second, the next batter, the veteran backup first baseman, Mark Yudof, stroked another single, this time to right field in the hole between the first and second basemen. The runner on second had a good jump with the pitch and scored easily, making it 7 to 4, Cubs' favor.

When the seventh Cub run crossed the plate, Red Trickey, in his characteristic style, turned the crowd microphone way up without saying anything for a full forty-five seconds. The noise of the crowd crackled loudly through the old RCA radio's Morning Glory speaker and blended nicely with the shouts and laughter coming from Lloyd Stevens' living room, porches, and pickup bed.

Lloyd watched as his son tossed his grandson gently in the air several times in a row to his grandson's great delight. Lloyd was beginning to think that this could be the year of finally winning the elusive division crown.

After Mark Yudof was at bat, the Reds' manager changed pitchers again. The next relief pitcher made short work of the Cubs' rookie catcher and rookie shortstop, striking them both out on 1–2 counts.

Still, it had been a good inning, and after five complete, the Cubs were ahead 7 to 4 with Hooks Harrigan still on the mound.

Lloyd Stevens and his guests anxiously listened and watched as neither team scored in the sixth and seventh innings.

In the top of the eighth inning, Hooks was scheduled to face the 3, 4, and 5 hitters for the Reds. He gave up a leadoff single, followed by a bloop double that scored a run before settling down to retire the side, making the score 7 to 5, Cubs, after 7½ innings of play.

As they had done previously during the course of the game, the Cubs answered with a run of their own in the bottom of the eighth from the bottom part of their order. Going into the ninth inning, the Cubs were up 8 to 5.

Everyone at Lloyd Stevens' house was excited and nervous as the ninth inning opened. Except for a few women monitoring a hide-and-seek game in the front yard, both porches, Lloyd Stevens' pickup, and all rooms of the house had emptied into the living room. Everyone was watching the television and listening to the radio intently as Red Trickey described what happened next.

Chapter 14

"WELCOME BACK TO THE TOP of the ninth inning at Wrigley Field where the Chicago Cubs are in command with an 8 to 5 lead, three outs away from claiming their first ever division championship in the history of the franchise. I suspect that no hot dogs or cokes are being sold at any of the stadium's concession stands at the moment because every seat in the house is taken as the Chicago faithful hold their collective breath in hopes that this is the year they finish ahead of their arch rival, the Cincinnati Reds, to claim the elusive division title.

"In something of a surprise move, Russ Freeman has apparently elected to start the inning with Hooks Harrigan still on the mound. Hooks has pitched brilliantly in relief since the fifth inning, after giving up two runs on the first pitch he threw. He finished strong last inning, so Russ has decided to leave him in there to try to finish the game.

"Ordinarily, we would see the Cubs' closer, Bill Buxley, in this situation; but, as many of you know, Bill is still nursing a sore right leg from the airplane crash two days ago. I see him warming up in the bullpen, and he appears to be all right, but I was told before the game that he is doubtful.

"With Hooks scheduled to face the 8, 9, and 1 batters for the Reds, Russ is hoping that the veteran reliever can finish the game and maintain the current three-run advantage.

"Hooks has completed his warm-up tosses. There goes the throw to second as the Reds' number 7 batter steps into the box. Fasten your seat belts out there in radio land. Here we go.

"Hooks looks in for the sign and begins his deliberate windup. Heeere's the pitch.

"The batter takes an aggressive swing, and the ball is hit weakly down the third base line. Guns Gleaton charges the ball and picks it cleanly with his throwing hand and fires to first on the run. Mark Yudof reaches down and digs out the throw, but not before the runner crosses the bag safely for an infield hit.

"Well, the Reds have a little something going to start the ninth. Guns Gleaton was guarding the line, and he made a good play on the ball once he got to it. The swing was so ferocious that Gleaton's first step was backwards and not forwards toward the slow roller. That first step backwards was all the advantage that the fleet-footed batter needed to beat the throw.

"Russ Freeman has not stirred from his seat in the dugout. Had that ball been hit sharply, we probably would see a pitching change now. But, you really can't fault the pitcher for that seeing-eye single.

"Ace Simmons, the Reds' manager, is going to his bench for the next batter. Pinch-hitting for the Reds will be the veteran backup first baseman, Jackson Smith. Smith is still taking warm-up swings next to the plate with a doughnut weight on the end of the bat. He removes the doughnut, flips it in the general direction of the bat boy, and steps toward the batter's box.

"Meanwhile, activity continues in the Cubs' bullpen with the regular closer, Bill Buxley, throwing by himself.

"Hooks Harrigan looks in for the sign, glances to first at the runner who is not a threat to steal in this situation, and comes to the plate. High. Ball one.

"The crowd got quiet after the opening infield hit and they're becoming a bit restless as they bite fingernails, chew gum, and shout encouragement to Hooks Harrigan as he prepares to make his second pitch to the inning's second batter.

"Hooks rocks and fires. There is a sharply hit ball into right field between the first and second baseman. The runner at first was off with the crack of the bat, and he'll easily make it to third. Jackson Smith applies the brakes at first with his pinch-hitting job completed well done. He'll be replaced by a pinch runner as Hooks holds his head down, staring at the ground behind the pitcher's mound. Time has been called.

"This is the situation that Russ was hoping to avoid. It looks as if he is going to try to use the injured Bill Buxley, but Russ has not signaled for him yet as he walks out to the mound. He now motions to the bullpen where Bill Buxley takes one more throw before departing for the pitcher's mound.

"Hooks Harrigan has pitched well in relief and it's a shame that he cannot finish this game. The crowd is still abuzz as they watch the Cubs' closer make his way to the infield with a disguised but, to the discerning, noticeable limp.

"There is an unwritten rule in baseball that batters don't bunt against an injured pitcher, but this might be the day that rule is broken if the right situation develops.

"As Bill Buxley steps to the mound, Hooks hands the ball to Russ Freeman, who completes the ritual by handing the ball to the new reliever.

"Listen to the hand this appreciative crowd gives Hooks Harrigan as he walks off the field and into the dugout, doffing his cap as he disappears from view.

"Thanks to our sponsors we'll keep it right here as Bill Buxley completes his warm-up tosses. In spite of his irregular gait as he walked to the mound, his pitches appear sharp and with sufficient velocity. His injured right leg, of course, is the one he pushes off with as he throws, but he seems to be holding his own as he completes his warm-up throws under the watchful eye of his manager.

"Fats Fitzsimmons is walking slowly to the mound. Pudge Jones is listening along with Bill Buxley to some last-minute instructions from Russ Freeman. As a matter of strategy, no pinch hitter has been announced, but I'm sure we'll see someone bat for the scheduled number 9 hitter. With a right-hander on the mound, we'll likely see another right-handed batter. There are three right-handed swingers remaining on the bench to select from, the most likely candidate being Julio Vasquez, who has led the National League in pinch hit doubles for the last 2 years.

"As Russ trots off the field, Julio Vasquez steps out of the dugout to the on-deck circle as expected to pinch hit. There are runners on first and third with no one out.

"The crowd is beginning to increase the noise level again as Julio stands in for the pitch. The book on Julio is that he is a first-ball hitter, and he's also known as a bad-ball hitter. It's difficult to completely waste a pitch on him without running the risk of throwing a wild pitch. With runners at the corners, don't look for a ball in the dirt.

"Here's the windup and the pitch.

"The ball is hit sharply into the gap in right field. The runner on third scores easily as Tonic Tisdale dives and keeps the ball from rolling to the wall. He rights himself and throws hard toward third. The ball is cut off by the shortstop as the lead runner slides into third. Julio Vasquez retreats to first as the ball is cut off, and he slaps his hands together and clenches his fists, exhorting his teammates to keep the rally going.

"One run has scored, making it 8 to 6, Cubs. But now, there are runners again at the corners with still nobody out and the top of the Reds' lineup coming to bat. Julio Vasquez is not a particularly fast runner, but he is a smart base runner. He will stay in the game and run at first base.

"The crowd noise has completely died down. At the beginning of the inning, the concession stands were empty because everyone was in the bleachers standing, stomping, and yelling for three outs to end years of frustrating baseball history in the Windy City.

Now the concession stands are still empty, but mainly because the home crowd is too nervous to eat or drink.

"Bill Buxley is looking to his dugout. Russ Freeman looks down to the Cubs' bullpen, where three pitchers are warming up. Russ makes no move to replace Buxley.

"The score is 8 to 6, Cubs, but the leading run is stepping to the plate in the form of the Reds' leadoff hitter. There are runners on first and third with nobody out.

"Pudge Jones glances into the Cubs' dugout to pick up the pitch selection signaled in from Russ Freeman as Bill Buxley toes the rubber, takes a deep breath, and stares toward the plate for the sign. It is hard to imagine any pitch other than pure heat in this situation as Bill begins his pitching motion, rocks, and fires . . . It's strike one.

"The Chicago crowd has had very little to cheer about in this inning thus far, but they roar their approval for that small taste of success and a 0 and 1 count. There is still no indication that Buxley is hurt as he pitches. That last pitch was clocked at 95 miles per hour, so his velocity is unaffected by his crash injury.

"Buxley is looking in again for the sign. Everybody in the park is expecting another fastball as he winds and throws. Tommy Thompson swings and misses for strike two. Again, the crowd roars its approval while Thompson steps out of the batter's box, places the bat between his legs, and goes through his painstaking ritual of tightening and retightening his batting gloves. Thompson is unquestionably the most deliberate batter in baseball, and he takes enormous amounts of time between pitches. As most of you know, his nickname in the National League is 'The Human Rain Delay.'

"Buxley is hardly paying either runner any attention because neither is a real threat to go in this situation. He is working, however, from the stretch position in order to keep them fairly close to the base. The count stands 0 and 2 as Thompson finally steps back to the plate. The crowd is now standing as Buxley prepares to throw the next pitch.

"He rocks and fires. The batter swings late and hits the ball foul down the first base side. The Reds' first base coach makes a nice play, inspects the ball, shakes his right fist that holds the ball, and flips it out of play and into the first base dugout. He might have seen a scuff mark on the ball, but many times, an opposing coach will seize an opportunity to get a ball out of play when a pitcher is in a good groove with the hope of slightly changing the pitcher's feel and rhythm of the game.

"The home plate umpire, Fats Fitzsimmons, throws a new ball out to the mound with his patented sidearm delivery and Bill Buxley begins the process of rubbing down the new ball behind the mound. While off the pitching mound, he goes to his mouth and adds saliva to his efforts to improve his grip for the next pitch.

"Meanwhile, activity continues in the Cubs' bullpen with three pitchers continuing to warm up in spite of the fact that Bill Buxley has thrown three consecutive pitches in the strike zone.

"Buxley now seems satisfied with the new ball, replaces the glove on his glove hand, and steps back toward the rubber. He shakes off a sign, nods approvingly at the second suggestion, pauses in the stretch position, and throws. Thompson swings and misses for strike three! Buxley surprised everyone, including the batter, with a slow changeup curve on that last pitch.

"There is now one out in the top of the ninth. Runners are still at the corners and Merv Wallace is coming to the plate. Listen to the crowd!

"Merv Wallace has batted .325 with runners in scoring position this year, but Buxley cannot afford to consider working around him here. To walk Wallace would mean loading the bases and looking squarely at the meat of the Reds' order with the 3, 4, and 5 hitters due up next.

"The score is still 8 to 6, Cubs. The runners at first and third have increased their leads with the lack of attention shown to them as Buxley winds and throws. It's a fastball that the batter hits weakly to the third base side. Buxley dives toward the third base line but is unable to field the ball cleanly. The ball rolls off his glove toward third base, where the third baseman fields it, but he has no play. All hands are safe, and the runner at third, who took off at the sound of the bat, scores easily, making it 8 to 7, Cubs.

"Bill Buxley, who lunged at that ball as it bounced slowly toward the shortstop, is still down clutching his right hamstring. I'm not sure he's getting up. He may not be able to continue.

"With runners at first and second and the score 8 to 7 and only one out, one of the three pitchers warming in the Chicago bullpen may be asked to come into the game and inherit a difficult situation.

"I'm looking through the binoculars at the bullpen to see if I can tell who is warming up. While most eyes are focused on Bill Buxley, who is being attended by the Chicago trainer, the three bullpen pitchers are throwing in earnest now. The left-hander is Lefty Daniels, who is normally the team's long reliever. One of the right-handers is Jules Vincent, who is rumored to have a sore arm. The third pitcher warming up in the deepest part of the park is . . . Henry 'Fast Ball' Harvey."

Chapter 15

WHEN JULIO VASQUEZ GREETED BILL Buxley's first offering with a sharp line drive to right field, Henry Harvey's and Russ Freeman's eyes met briefly in the Chicago dugout. Without a word, Fast Ball retrieved his glove from the equipment storage part of the dugout and made his way almost unseen to the Cubs' bullpen. Hooks Harrigan walked with him. Ostensibly, they were going to help prepare the remaining relief pitchers for the possibility of entering the game.

Immediately upon arriving in the bullpen, Fast Ball and Hooks began playing catch. After a few minutes, Hooks traded his fielder's glove for a catcher's mitt and Fast Ball began throwing in earnest. Far away in the dugout, Russ Freeman could see Fast Ball throwing hard on his own along with two other pitchers that Russ had ordered to be prepared to come into the game.

By the time Bill Buxley lay sprawling in the infield with a pulled hamstring in his already-injured right leg, Fast Ball was beginning to perspire from his efforts at limbering up his arm. Hooks' glove hand was red from the warm-up efforts.

When Russ realized that the extent of Bill's injury would prevent his continuing in the game, Russ took a long, slow look toward the Chicago bullpen. He motioned with his right arm.

There were two right-handers warming up, Jules Vincent and Fast Ball.

No one was sure which one he wanted, but no one objected, including Russ, when Fast Ball took one last warm-up toss and then turned to walk out of the bullpen gate and onto the playing field.

Bill Buxley was limping off the field, largely under his own power, just as Fast Ball arrived at the mound. The applause for the injured Chicago closer grew louder and then rose into a deafening crescendo as Fast Ball took the mound.

Russ looked into his old friend's eyes. Russ was not sure he was making the right decision. He suspected that the statistical sheets left behind in the dugout would have no record of Fast Ball's making a relief appearance. In fact, Fast Ball had not pitched in relief since the 4A high school playoffs in Texas over 23 years ago.

Although this was probably his most pressure-packed decision as a manager, Russ was oddly calm. He knew the hard part of making the decision about who to bring in was over. Now, he was a spectator, eager to watch the conclusion of a thrilling game that would signal the end of a season for one team.

Russ said, "There's one out, runners on first and second. We are still up by one with the good part of our order due up in the ninth. You know as much about the next few hitters as I do, so I'm going to let you and Pudge call your own pitches. Good luck."

"Thanks," said Fast Ball. "I'll see you in the interview room when I'm done."

Russ turned and walked away.

Under the rules of baseball, if an umpire determines that a pitcher is injured and unable to continue, the substitute pitcher has unlimited time to warm-up before play is resumed. Fats Fitzsimmons confirmed this ruling to Fast Ball and to Russ. He also advised the Reds' manager of the extended warm-up opportunity, but Fast Ball was almost ready to go after a brief strategy discussion with the infielders and his young catcher companion. Fast Ball threw only eight pitches to get accustomed to the mound.

After his last warm-up throw, he took off his glove and put it under his left arm as he walked behind the pitcher's mound and rubbed up the baseball. Noise was all around him, but his world was one of quiet concentration. He felt good. He was ready as he stepped to the rubber. He glanced at the runner on first base and looked out of the corner of his right eye toward the runner on second.

After an exaggerated pause at the top of the stretch position, Fast Ball counted silently to three, took his foot off the rubber, wheeled 180 degrees in a counterclockwise motion, and fired the ball to second on a timing pick-off attempt. The runner at second was clearly surprised, as was everyone else in the park including the second base umpire, but somehow the runner managed to dive headfirst back toward the bag with enough quickness to nurture a delayed safe call from the closest umpire to the play.

A chorus of boos erupted from the stands. Russ Freeman walked to the top of the dugout and glared at the second base umpire. Russ gestured toward Fats, but he did not step onto the playing field. He did not want to interrupt Fast Ball's rhythm and the flow of the game.

Fast Ball ignored the boos and immediately forgot about the call. He had accomplished his purpose. The runner at second would not be venturing too far off the bag again. That might be important before the inning was over. Also, the batter had been distracted.

As the boos continued from the crowd, Fast Ball again began his preparation to throw his first pitch. His initial offering was an inevitable fastball over the outside part of the plate for a called strike one. The boos were replaced by cheers.

Everyone was standing again in the stadium. Even some of the injured Cubs' players in wheel chairs in the overflow dugout were standing with the aid of crutches and the shoulders of teammates.

Fast Ball calmly waited for the batter to resume his stance in the batter's box. When the batter was set and had completed three warm-up swings, Fast Ball looked to first, peeked to second where the runner was only eight feet off the bag, and threw home. It was a perfect changeup curve on the inside part of the plate. The batter swung at the pitch but was way out in front of it. His swing was already over before the ball reached the plate.

The scoreboard registered the second strike for a 0 and 2 count as the stadium organist played the refrain from a popular song that had been written about Fast Ball shortly after his last career no-hitter. The red neon light decibel meter adjacent to the scoreboard high in left field registered a maximum 10 as Fast Ball looked in for the sign before the 0 and 2 pitch.

Every child and adult in the home team crowd stomped their feet in an ever-quickening cadence as the next pitch sailed toward home plate. The batter swung and missed a high fastball over the inside black of the plate. The stadium almost crumbled from the vibration of stomping feet and yells.

With the swinging strike three, there were now two outs and two still on base. The score stood 8 to 7, Cubs' favor. The cleanup hitter for the Reds, Oak Hogan, was coming to the plate.

Although everyone else in the Cubs' dugout was standing, Russ was sitting in his usual spot. He still felt calm and confident as he surveyed the crowd. It was a wonderful scene, and he was content as he watched and listened.

Russ glanced up to the press box and saw Red Trickey, who was standing and holding a microphone. He surveyed the TV cameras, the newspaper reporters, and the still-life photographers.

Although he felt as if his managing decisions were over for the night, he checked his statistics out of habit and saw that the Reds' cleanup batter sported an unusually high .323 lifetime batting average against Fast Ball. He did not need his records to know that Oak Hogan led the majors in home runs this year with 52 round trippers. Over half of them were against right-handed pitchers.

The reality of those numbers temporarily erased the poetry and magic of the moment in Russ's mind. Everything was happening in slow motion to Russ, but his inner calm was replaced by anxiety as he stood to watch the next at bat with his fellow coaches and the players.

On the mound, and in spite of his experience in pressure situations, Fast Ball was fighting hard to maintain his concentration. While facing the first batter, all of his powers of concentration were sharply focused on each pitch. Now, however, his thoughts were beginning to blur. Images of Madge, Russ, Deep Pockets, and his children were colliding in his mind's eye as he began to notice how noisy it was.

He backed away from the rubber. He then stepped back into his pitching position while the major-league's leading home run hitter stared toward the mound.

Fast Ball began his delivery and unleashed a high hard slider over the first base side of the plate.

The deafening noise turned to silence as Oak Hogan took a mighty swing and hit a towering fly ball toward the right field bleachers. With two outs, both base runners were off at the crack of the bat. Fast Ball watched helplessly as the ball sailed up and away from the infield in fair territory.

As Russ watched from the dugout, he had a sinking feeling because he had not replaced Tonic in right field at the top of the inning with a defensive specialist having better speed. Russ had thought he might need Tonic's bat in the bottom of the ninth. It was beginning to look as if he was correct about needing to score again as the ball headed toward the right field stands.

A commercial jet flew directly overhead as Tonic turned and ran toward the fence after the ball was hit. He had been playing deep so he was able to quickly cover the remaining ground to the wall. At full speed, he perfectly placed the tip of his left shoe into one of the chiseled out dents in the wall that he had carved over the years with his pocket knife. He used the extra leverage to jump up and extend his glove hand above the top of the outfield wall.

Fast Ball saw his friend's glove disappear over the wall with the momentum of his leap. After that, he saw Tonic fall to the grass in the outfield. The center fielder had raced to right field to back up the play, and he was looking for the ball.

The first base umpire had run toward the outfield wall to get a better view of the play. Just as the umpire was about to signal home run, Tonic raised his glove, showing the ball to the umpire. The umpire signaled out. The game was over. The Cubs had won 8 to 7.

Epilogue

BEFORE JOINING FAST BALL, TONIC, and Hooks in the interview room after the game, Russ went to his office and retrieved one of the photographs that Jamatsu and Flash Cube had made earlier. He got a black ink, felt-tipped pen and scratched through the word "Division" and wrote in the word "Pennant" so that the photograph now read "The Crash-Landing Cubs, National League Pennant Champs."

He took the touched-up photo out to the celebrating players, stood on top of a chair, and held up his hand for quiet. He told them that he wanted them to enjoy the moment, but he also said they had unfinished business. He then held up the photo and read the revised caption. Everyone exploded with shouts. Russ held up his hand again and told the players to be at the stadium for practice in the morning at 9:45 sharp.

Russ, Fast Ball, Tonic, and Hooks then headed for the interview room, shoulder to shoulder.

The Cubs won the National League Pennant in the following six games and went on to win the World Series in the seventh and deciding game against the Yankees with, you guessed it, Henry "Fast Ball" Harvey on the mound.

"WHEN EVERYONE LOVED THE GAME" **

There are things that I remember
  from a long time ago.
Some are dark and partly cloudy,
  some are white and clear as fallen snow.

I can remember my grandpa
  when he set me on his knee
And told me all about
  the things that I could be.

I remember when my grandma
  would drive us all to town
On a two-lane country road
  with wildflowers all around.

When a car would come toward us,
  she would cut the engine off,
And the neighbor from down the way
  and my grandma, they would talk.

I remember when my dad would go
  to see the neighbor's calf
And the owner of that ranch and
  my dad would have a laugh.

I recall choosing sides to play
  baseball in the street,
And I remember when kids from down the road
  would drop by to compete.

I remember filling stations
when your windows would get washed
As you pulled into the drive,
and asked a man you knew to fill'er up.

But this morning when I read the paper,
I realized that most things are not the same.
But I can still remember
when everyone loved the game.

www.ingramcontent.com/pod-product-compliance
Lightning Source LLC
Chambersburg PA
CBHW071402170626
46811CB00003B/1234